School

ISABEL PABÁN FREED

The author is grateful for permission to use quotes from works from Routledge, International Publishers, MIT Press, Stanford University Press, University of Texas Press, Duke University Press, Princeton University Press, Zer0 Books, and Penguin Random House.

Paperback: 979-8-9883234-2-6
Ebook: 979-8-9883234-1-9

Cover art: Zhanpei Fang
Proofreading: Avery D'Agostino

bartleby.life

For the petty bourgeois

Housekeeping

We eat people here. Basically nobody objects. You get used to things. Also, when you think about it, it's not that weird: we don't kill them. We wait until they're dead, and then, if they're good, we eat them. So it's not that weird. Or that allegorical. We know what it looks like. But we told her . . . we wait.

Otherwise, though, basically everything else is the same. You should be set. Enjoy!

Friday

They seem anxious . . .
— KARL MARX

Lunch

Lowering his fork and frowning at his phone:

> — Y'all see this?

> — What?

> — Self-immolation, Main Quad.

> — What?   — What?   — What?

> — Yeah.

> — When?

> — Dunno, must've been this morning, video's only been up for a bit. Look, — he says, holding out his phone, — it's-

> — Fuck.

> — She's . . .

> — Naked.

> — Yeah.

> — So . . .

> — Calm.

> — Yeah.

> — Fuck!

> — . . .

> — You think it's real?

He pulls the phone away.

— Dunno, looks real. That's definitely Main Quad.

— Where'd you find it?

— Came in an email.

— Someone you know?

Shaking his head,

— Bunch of letters and numbers.

— How many views does it have?

— . . . six.

— Anyone been to Main Quad this morning?

— Just got up.

— Same.   — Same.   — Same.

— Hmm . . . I'll text Jess, she should be in the Math building.

— Can you send me that link?

Nodding,

— Yeah one sec one sec she's typing . . .

— . . .

— . . . she says her class got canceled right before it was supposed to meet, says the professor didn't really give a reason, just said they would reschedule. Weird . . . alright, here.

— Thanks.

A little eating.

— So what do you think was this girl's like . . . mission?

— Her mission?

— Yeah you know you like . . . like if you're going to go and do something like that you gotta have like a . . . cause.

— Didn't look like she had a sign or anything.

— She could've left a note.

— Or a manifesto.

— Are people still manifesto-ing?

— Dunno, maybe it was like a performance art thing. Like with fake fire.

— Fake fire?

The door to the dining hall opens.

— Yooooo, what's good!

— Oh . . . hey Chip.

— What's uh . . . — he says, reading the room, — who died?

— No one knows.

— What?

— You been to Main Quad today?

— No, why?

— Someone-

— Video's down.

— What?

— Look, — she says, holding her phone out, — it's doing that thing where it's just static.

— 'This video has been removed because its content violated the Terms of Service agreement . . . ' Fuck.

— What happened in Main Quad?

— Someone like . . . immolated there.

— They what?

Miming,

— *Whoosh*.

— What like as part of Carneval or something?

— No one knows.

— Shit.

— Yeah.

— And there's a video?

— Not anymore.

— Shit!

— Yeah.

— Someone'll repost it, I'm sure.

— Man you guys don't think . . .

— What?

— Like . . . I'm supposed to give a tour today? You don't think they're still going to make me . . . do it?

— Fuck.

— Check your email, they just sent out an alert.

— Fuck me, listen to this: 'Students be advised, a combustive incident occurred early this morning in the Main Quad.' More or less slamming the table,

— 'Combustive incident'? — she says, hands now fully airborne. — A '[fucking] combustive incident,' can you imagine going through all that just to be a combustive, FUCK.

— Leah that's my face you're uh . . .

— Right, sorry, but I mean it's just like GOD. This is so fucked. Someone sets themself on fucking fire and it's just, ugh, I can-not WAIT for our beloved Madam President to make a statement about how like University has this 'deep commitment to caring for the mental well-being of its students,' and then like, 'how in light of the recent tragedy which has befallen the University campus, as an Administration, we will commit ourselves to ensuring that there are more effective, robust mental health services available to the student body,' and then what, they're going to hire like one more person and maybe, *maybe* they'll name an underwhelming scholarship after her? It's bullshit. It's such bullshit.

— Should we riot? — Chip says, smiling at Leah and wincing slightly as a pair of daggers sail just wide of his ears. — Oh c'mon Leah, I mean it's just like what are they going to do?

— They can do something, — Leah says, eyeing the daggers wobbling in the wall behind Chip.

— Can they?

— Do you have any idea how much money they have? Billions, Chip, bill-ee-uns. University has an endowment bigger than the GDP of a small country, the kind of country which, I might add, their investments are currently at work fucking over in like forty-six different ways.

— Yes okay I'm sure we can all agree: we have lots of money and imperialism is bad, but that's not my point. I'm saying what can they really do?

— Pay our tuition.

— Yes but-

— Hire more therapists.

— Yes but-

— Ooh are we making demands?

— What about like . . . better housing?

— Better food.

— Free coffee.

— Free massages.

— The masses have spoken! — Chip says, fist held at neck height. — All I'm saying is we can divest all our money from whatever Bad Stuff it's in, and we can invest whatever's left into making University the most luxurious luxury resort it can be. But-

— But?

— But what is that going to change?

— We'll have divested our money from Bad Stuff and made University into, what was it, the most luxurious luxury resort it can be.

Deploying a pair of lackluster jazz hands,

— And hooray for praxis!

— Well what do you want them to do Chip?

— They can't do anything. That's my point. It's fundamentally a problem they can't solve.

— Ah yes . . . — says Leah, exchanging a knowing look with the rest of the table.

— Capitalism.   — Capitalism.   — Capitalism.
              — Capitalism.   — Capitalism.

— . . .

— . . .   — . . .   — . . .
                    — . . .   — . . .

— Whatever, it's true.

— Obviously. But you always do this shit Chip. You can't just write off everything anybody does because it doesn't end capitalism, like just because it makes *you* feel better about doing nothing doesn't mean-

— So I have to pretend cosmetic-

— You're already pretending! Sitting around waiting for other people to revolt is pretending. Like what do you think is going to happen? Everyone's just going to wake up one day and-

— Decide to end capitalism, yeah.

— *Ugh.*

— Leaaaah, — he says.

— What? — she says.

— Obviously I don't think that.

— What do you think?

— Well I think really only *most* people have to wake up and decide-

— CHIP!

But Chip's already disappeared, chuckling to himself as he skips the line and walks straight into the dining hall.

— . . . wants to co-opt revolutionary aesthetics and act like he's this big fucking radical just because he read like one . . .

— They sent out another email, — says Beau Chicory, looking up from his phone, — looks like they moved the Career Fair out of Main Quad 'due to unforeseen acridity.' Man, who writes this shit?

— There's a Career Fair today?

— Yeah.

— Oof, glad I never have to go to one of those again.

— Same.   — Same.   — Same.

Nodding in agreement, and thinking of the stack of resumes he still needs to print, Beau invents an excuse, stands up from the table, and says his goodbyes; grabbing his plate, his fork, his knife, and his cup—and stacking them all together— he rounds the bend at the end of the dining hall, tosses his fork and knife in the overflowing bin, forgets to compost, and places his plate and cup on the outstretched hand of that giant, revolving apparatus, which carries his dishes away as Beau returns to the table, grabs his backpack, and steps out of the dining hall, emerging at last into the dull breeze of another glorious University day.

After some freak late-spring rain, the sun is back; the clouds have been taken down; the puddles dried out; the colors reinstalled—yes, it's safe to say, brochure weather has arrived: talk of the fabled University weather machine fills the air as students of all stripes take to perfectly manicured lawns, tossing aside readings and psets, stretching themselves out, yawning; others are in the midst of setting up elaborate drinking games, exercises in advanced cup topology whose rules the uninitiated will just have to hope do indeed totally make sense when you see it played; others still are tossing frisbees; playing cornhole; setting up hammocks; rolling out towels; taking pictures; posting pictures; scrolling; just ahead, a volleyball game waits patiently for its final player to pull the trigger on a risky text, toss her phone aside, and join the game; and across campus, where the benches are a little more secluded, freshmen haul conspicuous boxes holding weapons-grade drug paraphernalia, smirking past locals and their children, their schedules empty, their minds clear, fingers pointing lazily at the group of students flying drones over the aptly named Lake Bog—in short, campus is alive again, and students everywhere breathe a collective sigh of relief: the weekend is here; tomorrow's Carneval.

And yet, here's Beau Chicory. Having fruitlessly turned out his drawers in search of something more employable than boardshorts, he stares at the bag of dirty laundry on his floor, feeling every flavor of human emotion perpendicular to relief. Fuck, he thinks.

Beau's stressed. And not without reason: he knows himself well enough to know that even after he's gone to this Career Fair, handed out the last of his resumes, networked away what's left of his sanity, and picked up all the free swag he can carry, nothing short of an immediate, impossible job offer is going to ease the deep anxiety he's already begun to feel, that intractable doom Beau feels every time he considers the rapidly approaching horizon of Real Life and the impossibility of moving back home.

It's been months now. The job hunt. The career fairs. What feels like hundreds of applications. A few interviews. Many competitive candidates. More experience. The right fit.

He's tired.

And it's Laundry Day.

It's been Laundry Day.

Fuck, he thinks.

So as he stands there, at the foot of his bed, his nose now probing a pair of dress pants, his brain making some hasty speculations about smells and airflows, it's all but natural that a new feeling moseys its way into the room: who else but Dread's on-again, off-again partner Regret, who, with its back to the bed, and its hands braced against that inexplicably high frame, launches itself upward, smacks its head against the wall, and with a sheepish rub, looks Beau right in the eyes, saying, more or less: but isn't this all *your* fault?

Beau considers this.

But no, not really, he thinks. He's overworked, and his family hates him, but none of that is on him. And besides, he reads books: he knows about structures. He knows that it's structures that shape our everyday life, structures that determine who wins and who loses, who panics and who laughs, who parties, who works, who gets hired and who is stuck here, on the weekend of Carneval, stressing. And yes, Beau knows that can't be the whole picture: after all, we aren't just inert atoms pin-balling around systems of oppression; we have wills; we're agent, alive, conscious; swept up in the great river of History, for sure, but also capable of swimming, no doubt. But the whole metaphor's fucked, Beau says to Regret (who's starting to realize it's in for a little more than it bargained for), the whole metaphor's fucked because the thing is History is also swimming in us: it's here, in our heads, fucking around. So listen. There are people who think we have this agent, alive consciousness capable of structuring the world around us, and there are people who think the structuring of the world around us makes up our agent, alive consciousness, but the answer is that it's both/and. It's always both/and! You can't just invert things once. You have to invert, and invert, and keep inverting— it's motion! *Everything* is motion. Everything is constantly changing and updating and growing and decaying and *moving*, the whole world's moving, and we're a part of that. We can be a part of that. We just have to invert back. You swallow the world, and then you boot it back out. I mean *fuck*, Beau says, out loud, glancing at his mirror, I'm living proof, right? Isn't that what being trans is? Taking your reality and making it legible. Inverting back. And at the end of the day all these structures and systems and shit, it's all just *people*, right? And we could all stop. Stop and do something different. Something that doesn't make us want to set ourselves on fire. We could; we probably won't, but we could. And you know that

that's what they're doing. The ruling class, I mean. Inverting. Just look around, he says, gesturing, this is all them, isn't it? and fuck me if being here doesn't mean I'm not supposed to be a part of it too, or would be, anyways. Fuck.

But the room is silent. Regret's gone. It's only Beau now. Beau and his pants.

He puts them on and takes a deep breath. Then he goes to the computer cluster, and prints some resumes, and gets on his bike, and pedals all the way to the Career Fair, where he dismounts, and locks his bike, and prepares to smile.

☐

A little bit later, in her second office, our dear Madam President stands at the window, looking out over Main Quad.

— We can do both, can't we Parker?

Her administrative assistant looks up from his computer.

— Madam?

— The students and the school. We can do both.

— Indubitably.

— …

— …

— Where are we on the statement?

— 'A deep commitment to caring for the mental well-being . . .' Though peradventure, if I might make a suggestion?

Turning from the window, she gestures a yes.

— I'd suggest that we push the pathos up to an 8, maybe even a 9. I'm looking at the data now; it appears that the stu-

dents have a certain antipathy for language they have deemed
. . . if you'll er indulge, 'PR horseshit,' which is to say the
students appear to have a certain antipathy for language they
have deemed 'robotic,' which is to say 'cold,' 'unfeeling,' 'calculating,' etc.

— 'Robotic' and 'calculating'?

— Yes, though I would caution that this is an incomplete
dataset . . . there have been some difficulties with the data
collection process as the students have evidently developed a
troublesome habit of covering their laptop cameras with little
pieces of tape, which, as you might imagine, has-

— Robotic and calculating.

— Yes, Madam.

She turns back, sighing.

— Those ungrateful little shits.

— . . .

— They have no idea.

— Decidedly not.

— . . .

— . . .

— Keep the pathos at a 6 and announce that we'll be holding another Campus Climate Town Hall. Throw in all the
usual stuff about openness, dialogue, voluntary student in-
put. How does that sound?

— Immaculate.

— What's the status on the video?

— As of an hour ago, the video has been removed and no
others uploaded.

— Do we have any idea who sent it?

— Security has assured me that they are pursuing all relevant leads.

— Any contact from The Board?

— Unceasing.

— Wonderful.

— I'm afraid so.

The phone rings.

— Office of the President . . . yes . . . yes . . . quite tragic, sir, quite tragic . . . pardon? . . . yes . . . yes, it has proved rather difficult to ascertain the identity of the er immolee as there were no identifying documents found on the site of the . . . yes . . . I believe so . . . if I might inquire as to where exactly you learned of this incident . . . I see . . . and your son Chip is a student at University? . . . I see . . . to the President, sir? — making eye contact across her desk — I am afraid the President is inhumanly busy at the moment, may I suggest a better time to call . . . I see . . . perhaps if I better understood the nature of your call . . . I see . . . unfortunately I am afraid that I was being quite sincere when I said the President was inhumanly busy . . . pardon? . . . I do believe I have some idea who you are, yes . . . I see . . . I can indeed . . . a *new* medical center, sir? . . . that would be quite generous but I am obligated to inform you that at present we have received a number of competing bids . . . I am afraid I cannot divulge that information . . . I see . . . that is exceedingly generous, sir, but I am bound by a certain er secratorial code . . . no, I am afraid I must insist that I both can and must refuse . . . yes . . . of course . . . if you contact our Human Resources division . . . yes . . . yes, sir, the students and faculty of University would be forever indebted to your exceptional generosity . . . yes . . . thank you, sir . . . good day.

— Vultures. Generous, generous vultures.

— Truly, Madam.

Moving to her desk,

— Where are we on the girl?

— At present, no suitable information has been found. Security removed the body and cleaned up the site. They have informed me that they will send word immediately if they discover anything salient.

— And the police?

— Security has advised that we keep this 'in-house' for the time being. Evidently The Board has been quite insistent that we-

— 'In-house'?

— Yes.

— We can't cover this up.

— They were quite careful to avoid using those words.

The President takes a moment to imagine how good it must feel to be able to scream.

— Anything in the news?

— Nothing. Some chatter on the students' social media but with the video down, nothing definitive. I expect we will see major traffic by Sunday as I believe tomorrow they will have their hands busy with Carneval.

The President laughs.

— What a nightmare. Contact The Board and tell them I'll be in my office.

— Excellent.

— And Parker?

— Yes?

— Don't forget to take lunch.

Blinking,

— Of course.

The President exits the room. Parker continues to work.

Early Afternoon

— So I guess what I'm saying is that he really hasn't been doing anything wrong. He's been telling all these girls exactly what he's expecting, and exactly what they should expect from him. I mean he's not leading them on or anything. He's communicating, right? Like exactly what he's supposed to be doing. But they're still getting hurt. And I know he comes to me because I'm his friend and he wants validation that he's doing the right thing . . . and he is, but . . . I don't know, maybe that just isn't enough, — says Nat Larb, looking at her drug dealer.

The two sit in a small, blue pickup truck parked in front of one of the dorms.

— Young love, — says Hank, the drug dealer, — now ain't that a hell of a thing?

— Must be.

Hank smiles at her. He is old and has kind eyes—a case study, Nat often thinks, in the positive, long-term effects of sustained marijuana use. She suspects that he is an excellent grandfather, although she does not know if he has grandkids, only a daughter, who comes up from time to time in their weekly parking lot conversations.

— Now, — says Hank, pulling out two large shopping bags, — the trim job on these guys . . . I'd say I did about a 93. You've still got a few big nugs but nothing too sizable, take a look and let me know what you think.

— Looks good to me.

— I've got a half-pound of the AC Kush here just like you asked. Go ahead and give that a smell.

— Smells good to me.

— And I've got a half-pound of the DC Kush, a half-pound of the LLC Kush, and a half-pound of the ROTC Kush. Now this ROTC Kush I got from my neighbor, so give it a try, and if you and your friends don't like it, just let me know and we can always swap it out for something else.

— Alright, sounds good . . . here you go.

Nat hands him two large wads of cash, each held together with a black hair tie. Hank takes the money and, lowering the sun visor a little, slips the money inside, letting the visor press it against the truck's ceiling.

— So back to the grind, huh?

— Back to the grind, — says Nat, stuffing the weed in her purple backpack and smiling at Hank. She thanks him, does a quick sweep for police, and, finding none, steps out of the car and makes her way to her dorm.

It's legal now, weed, at least, nominally. But thanks to some discrepancies between state, federal, and University law, and on account—Nat suspects—of some backroom deals between the weed companies and University PD, they've been cracking down on dealers lately, those loyal stewards of capital offering a crude solution to the problems posed by the organization Nat currently represents: The Order of Plugs (The Order, or TOP; formerly The Order of Connects, or TOC), a cabal of University alumni whose regime of soft power and good will has, for the better part of a few decades, ensured that the current University Plug, presently one Nat Larb, enjoys the lion's share of University weed traffic, not to mention a suite of other on-the-job perks: free weed, free papers, free glassware, an extensive alumni network, access to an industrial kitchen, gym membership, prorated therapy, lawyers.

It's a competitive position, and applicants are thoroughly vetted: each year, dozens of University's most ambitious stoners submit themselves to a series of challenges devised around The Order's Five Pillars: Consumption, Production, Fitness, People Skills, and Political Education, the first four of which were no problem for Nat, who easily outsmoked, outrolled, outran, and outchilled everyone in her weight class, but who nevertheless made the rookie mistake of sitting the written exam sober, and studying stoned, evidently having skipped the readings on state-dependent memory, a mistake which might have done her in had it not been for her exceptional vibes and diverse edible portfolio, both of which so thoroughly wowed The Order's judges that, for the first time in over a decade, the year's selection was made by unanimous vote—all to say that if anyone was prepared to take on Big Weed, and win, it's our Nat. And yet the sad truth is that exceptional vibes and soft power regimes can only do so much in the face of superior technology and venture capital, and even though Nat matches the convenience of home delivery, at competitive prices, there's no getting around the fact that texting a drug dealer for the first time is a source of considerable anxiety for many University students, who, it seems, would much prefer to simply download an app and have an anonymous delivery person dispatched to their door, no stress, no fuss, no lingering anxiety about doing something illegal, or embarrassing, no nothing, just clean, simple ease—something Nat resents, of course, and not just for personal reasons: it's not like you needed to do all the reading to see how fucked it all was: legalization was good, yeah, but the way they'd gone about it, communities still destroyed, millions still wasting away in cages, and the same people that put them there collecting their billions . . . fucked, so fucked.

Sighing, she sorts the last of the weed into its appropriate jar and checks her phone.

Josiah Tibs: Which isn't to say that I begrudge her for the way she feels, quite the contrary; it's just that it's frustra . . .

Josiah Tibs: Haven't heard anything back from Sarah, starting to think that I shouldn't have begun . . .

555-843-1783: Hi! Hope you're doing well! I heard from a friend that you might be able to help me get some . . .

Maryanne Ham-Cobbler: we're ready when u are, come thru binch

She'd help Josiah later. Business first.

□

There are four houses in University's sorority cluster. Three

are sororities; the fourth, Nat's home, is a dorm of little dis-
tinction, nestled away in the outskirts of East Campus and
known primarily for its chef and abundance of two-room dou-
bles. Nat enjoys both: she's a big eater, her roommate's an old
friend, and she likes having her space; still, she would've preferred something more central: cross-campus deliveries are a
time sink, and her dorm's a little too out of the way for people to stop by on their way back from class. There's no gaming
The Lottery, though, that arcane system University Housing
uses to assign each student their housing for the year. The Order has tried. But even they don't have enough clout, or tech-
nical knowhow, to crack The Lottery's defenses: a slew of so-
phisticated cryptographic algorithms, which rumor has it run
on prime numbers known only to University Housing; and
a tight-knit staff, scared into loyalty by threats greater than
death.

If you're merely participating, then The Lottery is fairly
straightforward. After freshman year, students enter in groups
as large as eight; they rank their housing choices; then each
group is pseudo-randomly assigned a number based on the
tier they use: 1, 2, or 3. Higher tiers get lower numbers; lower
numbers get first choice of housing; and after the year, the
tier is spent, which introduces a considerable level of strategy
into the decision, seeing as there are, of course, complications:
sororities, fraternities, co-ops, theme houses, ethnic houses,
staff assignments, study abroad, reassignment, and medical
accommodation all provide alternative routes into desired housing. And housing is desired, for good reason: a few years ago,
a team of University Housing researchers released an inter-

nal report showing that housing is the single largest determining factor in a University undergrad's social being; having tracked the movement of various capitals through the University campus, they were able to conclusively show that, a few community centers and extracurricular hubs aside, social capital flows were anchored around a particular set of houses, concentrated largely on the Row. In fact, the relationship between housing and social being was so strong that the researchers produced a series of statistical models they claimed could predict up to thirty-seven metrics about a student based on their housing choices alone (everything from academic success to preferred source of protein).

The report was eventually leaked and, by all observable metrics, the following year's Lottery was the most socially antagonistic period in University history, confirming what amateur University anthropologists have been saying for years, that the annual ritual of The Lottery is the epicenter of campus drama, a knife that pseudo-randomly strikes through the social fabric, leaving a trail of rent friendships in its wake. It's not uncommon, a few bowls in, to hear suggestions that this is no bug, that The Lottery is in fact a strategic system of social control meant to keep the student body divided, lest they start getting any big ideas … but such paranoia requires a deep faith in the competency of the University administration, and isn't it easier to think those in charge are just bumblers, bumbling from one gaff to the next? Who could believe such misery exists by design?

Whatever their reasons, the gods of The Lottery chose to place Nat close to the sororities, and this had its perks: for example, the patronage of one Maryanne Ham-Cobbler, who along with her twin sister Jolene, also a University student, also a voracious stoner, is heiress to the Cobbler and Ham fortunes, which had been multiplied by a messy political marriage into a considerable sum, some minute fraction of which is soon to enter Nat's hands, as soon as either Maryanne or Jolene remembers to check their phone.

— I think you should go for it!

— But what if she says no?

— Then she says no, and honestly, fuck her! It's not like you don't have other options.

— Yeah but none of them have anywhere near the funding she does.

— That's true.

— And she has all sorts of industry connections.

— That's true.

— And I like her.

— All true.

— Plus it's like exactly the kind of research I want to do. It's just like her lab never works with undergrads, and I feel like it'd be so presumptuous of me to ask.

— So? Jolene, c'mon. You deserve this. And if she can't see that then fuck her!

— You think?

— Of course.

— Oh . . . Nat's here. Should I get her?

— Yes binch.

A minute or two pass.

— . . . no real plans, I mean there's a bunch of parties but I don't know if I'll-

— NAT!!

— Hey Maryanne.

— Girl. You reek.

— You did ask for-

— Two ounces of that dank AC Kush, yes, which, I'm assuming, you . . .

— Yep, right here.

— Sweet, well here's this and . . . thaaank you, we will take great care of it, I promise. Do you have time for a quick J?

— I would but I got this study I'm a part of. Have to make sure I'm there by one, and sober.

— What sort of study is it?

— Psych and biochem. They needed someone with a history of drug use, and the money's good, so I figured.

— The right girl for the job. Well don't let us keep you. Jolene and I were just discussing her promising future as an underpaid research assistant.

— Potential future.

— Oh yeah? Which professor?

— B'ssara, in Bio-E.

— Oh no shit. She's the one that hooked me up with this study, actually. I could put in a good word for you if you wanted.

— Oh I don't want you to have to-

— It's my pleasure Jolene, really.

From behind a very large cloud of smoke,

— Natalie Larb, you are a pillar of this community.

— Yeah thank you Nat!

— Of course . . . oh it's getting close to one, I should head out. Lovely seeing you two, as always.

They say goodbye and Nat exits the room, retracing her steps through the sorority and eyeing the Carneval decorations: things are looking pretty yonic in Theta Delta Phi these days, she notices, walking past a sawed-off newel post; it's a little aggro, not that Nat (trans) especially minds, although maybe she should . . . but no time to linger: she's got places to be.

She gets on her longboard, and begins to cruise towards The Institute, thinking idly about all the stops she'll have to make before dinner: The Institute; back to her dorm to pick up the weed; then to see Carmen Quico in Burrata; Eddy Eggs in Molasses; Alyx Doogh way out in Colcannon; Jedidiah Slop in West Bog . . . fucking Jedidiah, she wasn't looking forward to that one; Kathleen Bisque over in the grad student housing; James Laziji, Taara Bhatura, and Eli Knish, her trio of freshman goons; Olive; the Degenerates; Brie; and then, at last, home, where she'd wait for Josiah to come over for dinner, a meal which would almost certainly be spent discussing whatever it was that was happening with Josiah and his love life.

But those are all problems for Future Nat. Present Nat just wants to cruise. Cruise, and soak. The sun. The breeze. The bike wheels whirring around her. Her therapist has told her to practice mindful walks, or mindful rides, in her case. To isolate a sense, and focus on it; empty her head. Just listen to the bikes. The feet hitting the ground. Wheels rolling on asphalt. People, talking. Their words just sounds. Or maybe to just feel the heat of the sun on her skin. The air rushing against her. The breeze going the other way. It works. She feels calmer. At ease. Empty, in a meaningful way.

It's only when she's like this that she finds she can really appreciate the campus, which, when vacated of all its stressors, anyone can see, is pretty nice: lush greenery and gorgeous, yellow sandstone; red roofs; blue skies; a nice place, if you can stand to forget a few things, like Nat has now, rolling up to the glass-and-steel monstrosity that is The Institute. She holds her ID up to the scanner and waits a half-step for the door to unlock, pulling when she hears the click.

Inside, she heads down a confusing series of hallways. She needs to get to the basement, or one of them, anyways, University legend having it that The Institute building extends deep into the bowels of the campus, and then some. But she knows where she's going. She's been here before. The lab's just three lefts, two staircases, and a right away. She opens the door.

— . . . the whole thing's just utterly psychotic, she's basically arguing that if you're a white, cisheterosexual male that you've already benefited so much that you should basically just shut up and get out of the way, which is just . . . psychotic, utterly psychotic, I mean it's like I'm in my tribe, you're in your tribe, and god forbid we share some common humanity that lets us- oh hello Natalie.

— You're talking about that op-ed?

— Yes. You've read it?

— No, just heard about it. I didn't know grad students

read The Rag.

— No, normally I don't but this particular polemic has been making the rounds. I was just telling Rachele here that the thing is just totally, utterly . . . well you must've heard me.

— She must've, — says Rachele Schmaltz-Prosecco, stifling a tremendous yawn, — ready for your drugs then, Nat?

— Really, — Ashton mumbles, as he shuffles away to retrieve the drugs.

— If you'll lie down on this table . . . great. So, how are things? — Rachele asks, as she wires Nat up to a series of sensors and monitors.

— Things are good. You know, more of the same I guess. Hard to complain. What about you?

— Oh everything's a total shitshow right now. You remember how I was telling you about my friend Jules?

— They're the poly one with the thing about the dog?

— Yeah, exactly, well, the dog thing totally blew up and now things are getting catabolic in the polycule, it seems.

— Oh no.

— Yeah, and since I'm basically friends with all of them, they're asking me to step in and mediate.

— An excellent opportunity to work on your interpersonal communication skills, — observes Ashton, having returned with the drugs.

— Sounds hard.

— Yes, but I relish the opportunity to work on my interpersonal communication skills. If you'll just give me your arm here for a second . . . great . . . you should start to feel that in a minute or two. Just close your eyes and relax, we'll see you when you come around.

□

— Something's not right.
— What do you mean?
— Look.
— . . .
— . . .
— Yes, that does seem strange. We've never seen numbers like that. Is it possible there was something else in her system?
— She seemed sober.
— Yes, but she did smell-
— I trust her, Ashton.
— Hmm.
— Maybe the sensor's broken.
— Doubtful.
— Did you get the dose right?
— Of course I got the dose right.
— And you're sure it was c-fentanylase? Can you pass me that vial?
He passes her the vial.
— Hmm.
— 'Hmm'?
— Well the thing is, Ashton, this says c-*fetish*nylase.
— Oh dear.
— 'Oh dear'?
— It would appear that I have made a mistake.
— That is how it would appear.

— FUCK! Fuckfuckfuck. This is . . . they'll pull our funding. That's . . . how are we supposed to . . . fuck . . . okay we tell no one, and we fudge the numbers.

— What?

— It won't be difficult, we create a simple model that simulates the distribution we've seen thus far and randomly draw from it . . . it shouldn't take more than a few hours. I can do it tonight. It'll have a minimal impact on the study as a whole, and if we do it right it will be impossible to tell. Yes . . . okay this is fine.

— What?

— It's simple, really. We assume a gamma distribution parameterized-

— Ashton, what the fuck? What about Nat?

— Oh . . . yes . . . her heart rate is normal. Theta waves stabilizing.

Nat gives a well-timed stir.

— There we go, practically awake already.

— Fuck.

— What?

— What do you mean 'what'? I have to tell B'ssara.

— You absolutely do not.

— Ashton if anyone finds out-

— It would be bad, yes. However, I'm sure they would be equally scandalized if they found out what you've been doing with that ergotamine that's oh-so-mysteriously disappeared.

— . . . how did you know about that?

— Just a hunch, but confirmed now.

— Fuck.

— So you see we're at an impasse.

— I do see that.

They both look at Nat, immobile on the table.

— Do we just wait?

□

After an hour of restful sleep, Nat wakes up.

— How'd I do? — she asks.

Rachele smiles weakly as she takes the sensors off of Nat's forehead.

— Exceptional, as always.

— Sweet. I'll see you next Friday, then?

— Sounds good. Do you want to stick around for a bit?

— I would, but I've got work.

Fully desensored, Nat gets up from the table. She walks towards the door, grabs her longboard, and maneuvers her way out of The Institute. A wave of classes is about to end. Nat breathes.

— Nat.

She looks over.

— Cal! Hey, long time no see.

Cal gestures at The Institute.

— Had a change of heart?

— Oh, not really, just participating in a study. Getting paid to do drugs, you know.

— I see, — he says, — haven't seen you around much this year.

— Yeah . . . I've got this new job that's been keeping me pretty busy.

— Yes, Bun mentioned something about that. And you've been enjoying it?

— What?

— The job.

—Oh, yeah, yeah a lot actually.

— That's good. — Cal pauses. — You seem good, Nat.

— Yeah. Yeah! I think I'm pretty happy.

— That's good. I'm glad to hear that.

— And what about you? How have you been, man?

— Oh, — says Cal, — about the same. Busy. Another 22-unit quarter.

— You've got big Carneval plans, then?

Cal smiles. The wave of classes has just ended. He checks his watch.

— I should get going, Nat. It was good to see you.

— Yeah, you too! Wanna get a meal sometime?

Cal looks at Nat, smiling again.

— Sure. You have my number.

— Sweet.

Cal departs, and Nat takes a minute to look around. It's a little overwhelming, isn't it? All these people. But she feels fine. Good, even. Good to see Cal. And it's pleasant, watching the streams of students leak out of the various buildings that encircle Main Quad, filling the streets; it all feels very alive; that's the word Nat would use: alive; the way her fellow students are moving; the way the trees are breathing in the breeze; alive; very alive. It's fun, she discovers, to imagine the University campus as an organic thing, a body, made up of various organs and cells; the students would have to be the cells, of course; the roads the veins; the . . . departments the organs? or maybe the houses; it depends how you look, Nat supposes, because it could also be the communities; there were options, for the organs; but the students were the cells, the roads were the veins, Nat felt good about that much. So what did that make her? Was there a type of cell that shuttled chemical compounds around the body? At this thought, Nat feels a spasm of pride. She likes having a place. And she likes her stoners. Always has. Plus it's not like she doesn't have other friends. Cal. Josiah. Ah. She should probably respond to those texts.

She pulls out her phone. Weird. There's a bump on the screen. She prods it with her finger, and the glass jiggles, like jelly. She blinks. Is it getting bigger? She blinks again. The bump is definitely getting bigger. She looks back at The Institute, and then around at the other students. Everything seems normal. She looks at her phone.

The bump is clearly getting bigger, and she can see that it's extending toward her. Some cracks have started to appear in the glass, and now it's falling away in chunks, exposing what looks like a finger. A finger is coming out of her phone. A gloved finger covered in dirt. A gloved finger covered in dirt followed by a few more gloved fingers covered in dirt, forming a gloved, dirt-covered hand, which is attached to a wrist, which is attached to an arm, which is all getting dangerously close to her face. Nat drops the phone, and the hand extends even further into the sky as an elbow appears and then another arm and then both arms bend downwards, placing their hands on the ground and pushing until shoulders appears and then a neck and then a head and then a helmet, and then a chest and a torso and then both knees, along with attached legs and boots, which are on the ground now. The man stands up, stays there for a second, and promptly collapses.

Nat takes a step away from her phone, staring at the man. What the fuck? Why did a miner just crawl out of her phone? She looks at the phone again. Another hand is groping its way out of the screen. This one is faster. She watches, transfixed, as another miner emerges from the phone. And then another. And then another. And then the bodies start to come in twos and threes and fours, erupting out of the phone. Some are miners; others wear masks and white hats, only their fingers encased in rubber gloves; some look like they worked on ships; others wear company-branded hoodies and carry heavily stickered laptops. The bodies are a blur now, rocketing out of the phone too fast for Nat to examine.

Some of the other students have noticed Nat staring at the phone on the ground. Someone walking by asks if she's okay, but Nat can't acknowledge them. She's too busy looking at Main Quad, which is just sweating bodies. They're falling out of the walls and tumbling out the windows; the ground is littered with them, and now they seem to be sprouting bodies of their own: women, mostly, although there are a few men. She starts to move, trying not to look at the bodies ballooning out of the bikes swerving around her, or the ones dropping from the trees. Something's at the bottom of her vision. She looks down. A spider of arms is protruding from her shirt. Small arms. Children's arms. She feels nauseous. There's a bathroom hidden away behind one of the buildings. She stumbles toward it, flinging open the door, and looking down the steps at the row of stalls, which are, of course, overflowing with bodies. She can't. Bodies leaking out the faucets, bodies pressing out the mirrors, bodies from the tiles, bodies from the walls. She pukes. Chunks of food splatter across the stairs, and from them, more bodies: farm workers, slaughterhouse workers, truck drivers, her dorm's chef.

She goes down the steps and into the emptiest-looking stall. She locks the door. She just needs to breathe. In, and out. In, and out. She shuts her eyes. Breathe. Breathe. It's going to be okay.

She opens her eyes. But everything's black. She shuts her eyes again, and opens them, and shuts them, and opens them. Everything's still black. She gropes toward her eyes and thinks she feels a leg kicking out of her eye socket. Her contacts. She scratches at them but only succeeds in drawing a little blood, which dribbles down her face as she finally collapses on the floor of the stall, where she'll stay, immobile, wretched, fetal, and murmuring softly to herself until the door opens, and they come marching down the stairs.

Afternoon

Something is wrong with the heating in West Bog. It's too hot. Even here on the third floor, in the room with the blackout curtains, it's too hot. The pair of roommates watching TV are very sweaty, and neither of them has noticed that the laptop, roughly centered on the floor, with the HDMI cord coming out of its right side, and the AUX out its left, and the charger also out its left, and the external mouse again out the right, that this whole mess of cords and screens looks, to put a finger on it, a lot like they do, sprawled on the couch, in varying degrees of half-nudity. What they have both noticed is that unlike last week, there's a small, white X floating at the corner of an otherwise barely visible, semi-opaque gray box, where the illegal streaming site would have placed an ad had it not been for the third-party extension they have installed. But neither of them wants to get up to click it. If they did, there would be no hope of returning their body to the position it was in, and they're both feeling pretty good about where they are, as far as body positions are concerned.

This small, white X, though. It's really starting to get to the left roommate, who's now thinking seriously about the pros and cons of getting up, and really thinking about how they'd love it if the right roommate was the one to get up and go to the computer and click the small, white X, even though they, the left roommate, know that they, the right roommate, almost certainly won't, since they, the roommates, have been in situations like this before, and the right roommate has always opted for just letting things be, opted for stasis, which explains a lot about the right roommate, the left roommate thinks, and a lot about the room the roommates are currently in: things like the galaxy of popcorn kernels, chip dust, and lost weed swirling beneath them, under the couch cushions, and also the ants. It's not that big a deal, the cleaning; it's maybe only a big deal because the left roommate isn't actually that clean, which you'd know if you saw their room, it's just that when it comes to the common room, where the roommates spend most of their time, the left roommate likes for it to be clean, especially going into the weekend, when the roommates are sure to make a mess, or, at the very least, accumulate one.

Over in the right roommate's head, things are a little more tense. They've just come back from class, a creative nonfiction workshop, not even the kind of thing they'd normally take, but since they heard good things about the teacher from the left roommate, they decided to sign up for it anyway, something that had made sense at the time, and it's true that they had been pretty happy with the way the class was going, but then it came time to submit their main essay for the quarter, and, not knowing what else to do, they'd gotten pretty intimate and polemical about things like family and gender—a little out of character, but it felt right then; now it just seems embarrassing and trite, not the kind of thing they wanted twelve of their classmates to read, to say nothing of the teacher, which is why they're feeling so anxious right now—that, and it probably didn't help that after they came back from class, feeling anxious but nevertheless in the mood to celebrate the coming of Carneval weekend, they decided to finish off the last of their, the roommates', PVC Kush in a valiant attempt to get reasonably obliterated, which didn't work, not that it ever works, at least, not for the right roommate, though it does seem to work quite well for the left roommate, or so thinks the right roommate, who even after nearly a year of living together has honestly no idea what goes on in the left roommate's head, it being one of the great mysteries of the suite (the other being, of course, the existence of a squadron of malicious, kleptomaniacal gnomes, who periodically sweep—unseen—through the suite, stealing lighters, pens, and other valuables. This, the existence of the gnomes, is one of the few things the roommates agree on, along with the total abolition of gender, a few treasured TV shows, and an utter disdain for Leo, their third roommate, who mostly lives at his girlfriend's place).

God it's hot. The roommates exchange a look. A thick sweat haunts their inner thighs.

— Should we leave?

— Finish the episode, maybe.

On screen, a pair of friends discuss the day's plans:

— All I'm saying is when you get down to it, what's one less clown?

— Besides a capital offense?

— Oh, c'mon B., it's not like we're running into a birth-day party and shanking some dude making a balloon giraffe. These clowns are a menace. You watch the news, they're basi-cally terrorists.

B. snorts.

—A loosely organized group of twisted sadists using vio-lence and fear tactics to push an agenda? You tell me.

— In what world do these clowns have a political agenda?

— If you're always looking at the trees, B., how are you going to see the forest? We'll be doing everyone a favor.

— Yeah I'm sure his family and friends and-

— We're talking about a guy whose idea of fun is dressing up like a homicidal clown, the dude doesn't have a support network. Besides, he lives alone in the woods.

— Yeah?

— Yeah. It's a shithole. Look, even on the infinitesimally small chance that someone goes looking for this guy, and some-how the police pull their collective head out of their collective ass and trace it back to us, we just say we were out in the woods when some creep in a clown mask attacked us, one thing led to another, we killed him in self-defense, and we were too scared to report it.

— But why?

— What?

— Why would we kill him?

— Oh. I don't know, don't you think it'd be fun?

— Get the fuck out of my house, Dean.

— B., B., B., — Dean says, shaking his head, — you used to be so much fun, what happened?

— . . . what happened to this show?

— I have no idea.

— Weren't they in high school at some point? — says the left roommate.

— They still are, question mark? — says the right.

— I have no idea.

The show wraps up, and the roommates sit staring at the blank screen. The small, white X is still there.

— It's funny murder's illegal.

The right roommate looks at the left one.

— I mean, it should be, at least insofar as anything should be illegal. But it's not like that's what's stopping you from murdering someone. Like if they legalized murder tomorrow, I don't think you'd run around murdering people.

— No.

— And I don't think most people would run around murdering people.

— What about serial killers?

— What about them?

— Wouldn't they run around murdering people?

— Aren't they already running around murdering people?

The right roommate thinks about this.

— So you want to legalize murder?

— Decriminalize.

— Okay but if the law isn't stopping anyone from murdering, then what's the point? It shouldn't matter either way, right?

— I think it'd be like a symbolic gesture.

— What?

— Like we did it, mission accomplished. We can take off the training wheels.

— What?

— You know, — says the left roommate, hunting around for a lighter.

The right roommate looks at their phone. They've been sitting on a text from their boyfriend—nothing scary, the text is totally innocuous, an inside joke about a class they're taking together, but nevertheless, the right roommate is having trouble responding to it, in part because it's about the time in the conversation when they, the couple, should start figuring out their Carneval plans, and in part because at this present juncture in time, they, the right roommate, are finding it extraordinarily difficult to text, hypersensitive as they are to every one of the unintended meanings taken on by the drafts of their texts, which the right roommate is riskily writing out in the actual chat itself, and not in a separate app, something that has burned them before when they accidentally sent a draft text mid-edit, exposing not just the skeleton of their text, with all the various stock phrases they use jumbled in nonsensical order, but the fact that they draft their texts at all, which, cringe, not the kind of person the right roommate wants to be, and definitely not the kind of person they think their boyfriend wants them to be, so all things considered, maybe better to just let it be and respond later, when they've had some more time to think, and are a little less high.

— Are you hearing anything that I'm saying?

— What?

— Lmao, you weren't, okay, that's fine.

— Sorry, sorry. I was trying to respond to this text Xay sent me.

— Go ahead.

— No it's . . . not happening.

— Okay. I was saying we should get out of here. I'm thinking, The Tavern? Get some food, maybe a pitcher?

— Isn't dinner at 6?

— C'mon, get dressed, we're going out.

— What, I can't go like this?

— Babe.

— Kidding, kidding. I'll get dressed.

The roommates get up from the couch, into their clothes, and out the door, where it's considerably cooler, but also much brighter.

Over here on West Campus, things are a little more nature-y: the buildings are a little more spaced out, the trees a little rustlier, Lake Bog a little more extant. Normally the roommates would walk along the lake, but in the name of hunger, they've decided to opt out of the scenic route and are instead walking down one of campus's main arteries, a road clogged with bikes, skateboards, longboards, hoverboards, electric longboards, electric unicycles, cars, trucks, and pedestrians, all fighting for the right of way, which the left roommate is confident they have as they step out onto the crosswalk, looking, somewhat judgmentally, at the tour group on the other side of the street, whose guide is pointing at the building in front of them and explaining in great detail the University news ecosystem: the major players, their beefs and various financial backers, a subject which the tour guide clearly has great enthusiasm for, much to the dismay of most of the tour group, who just want to see Main Quad, and then ask questions about various admissions details, never mind the intricate complexities of the op-ed war being waged between The Institute-funded University Reviewed and the official school newspaper, The University Weekly, a third and fourth front of which, they're learning, has just opened up thanks to the emergence of a new, nominally leftist publication, The University Rag, and the usual antics being stirred up by that anonymous, muck-raking newsletter every student inexplicably receives in their inbox, The QuadSquad. But the tour group will have to endure a little more as the tour guide stays in front of The Weekly's building, where we should also probably stop, at least for a second or two, just to see what's going on.

□

— 'Bad Trip in the Quad'? Not really news, is it? What else we got?

— We've got the video.

— What video?

She holds out her phone.

— Ho-lee hell! And no one thought to show this to me sooner?

— Can't get any confirmation on it.

— What do you mean we can't get any confirmation on it?

— No proof that it happened here.

— We've got the email about the combustive incident but this video was posted *after* that was sent. Could be a prank.

— Hearing that this is a repost.

— Impossible to prove, though.

— Looks like Main Quad.

— It does look like Main Quad.

— What'd the administration say?

— Declined to comment except to say that they've seen the video and are preparing a longer statement, which we can expect sometime over the weekend, after Carneval.

— Why're they waiting so long?

— Who's going to read it tomorrow?

— Good point.

— Anything from QuadSquad yet?

Checking her phone,

— Doesn't seem like it.

— It's only a matter of time. They're going to report it, confirmation or not.

— A hundred percent.

— Fuck.

— So we're just supposed to sit on our ass until what, University admits that one of their students lit themselves on fire?

— Guess so.

— Fuck.

— What do we have in op-eds?

— STEM vs. humanities; humanities vs. STEM; tech is bad; tech is good; tech: a dialectical approach; support grad students; divest from fossil fuels; divest from the military-industrial complex; divest from the prison-industrial complex; divest from the international ivory trade; divest from tech; what's wrong with hoarding; let food trucks on campus; support grad students . . . or else; abolish the nuclear family; in defense of traditional marriage; what the humanities have to teach us about the beauty of mathematics; abolish Carneval; why identity politics fall short; why white vegans need to chill; why I chose to fail BIO 151; abolish The Lottery; abolish University Reviewed; staff selection: an empath's nightmare; University: a hedge fund with a small college attached; respecting our student workers; what the QuadSquad got wrong; it's not masculinity, it's men; ending the stigma: in defense of mayonnaise; University, the housing crisis, and you; self-care in a time of radical complicity; no, I won't just 'get out of the way;' abolish The Weekly.

—So more or less the usual, then.

— More or less.

Gesturing at the office phone,

— Give me that.

— What are you doing?

— What do you think? I'm calling up our dear Madam President.

— I already told you-

— Hello . . . yes, this is Mike Beef with the Weekly, may I speak to the President . . . inhumanly busy, got it . . . I'm calling about the combustive incident in the Main Quad . . . yes, I'm looking at a video now and if my eyes are not deceiving me, I'm watching a self-immolation in the Main Quad, care to comment? . . . Of course it's Main Quad . . . I don't have conclusive evidence, no, but anyone can see that . . . no, you listen to me . . . what do you mean it'd be most lachrymose to publish a false story . . . no I know what lachrymose means, I mean what do you mean . . . so you're saying you can neither confirm nor deny whether the video is real . . . right . . . yes . . . right . . . of course . . . but none of that means . . . no . . . well what does the President think . . . no, I know that you're going to issue a statement, I'm asking you . . . no . . . of course . . . thank you.

— I told you.

— So we're exactly where we started.

— More or less.

Mike Beef slams the table.

— Fuck!

□

Not great, but at least outside things are looking up. The left roommate's headed into The Tavern to secure a tower of fries and a pitcher of beer; the right roommate's stayed in the courtyard, looking for a pair of seats. The picnic tables are all full, but there's a four-seater in the back of the courtyard, perfect for the right roommate, who likes to be able to see what's going on: the people coming and going; groups of grad students huddled, conspiratorially, over pitchers of beer; loud boys engaged in a raucous battle of stories; undergrads working—or, at any rate, seeming to; the right roommate has their doubts that anyone can manage to get work done in this courtyard, though not for lack of trying, just it seems . . . un-likely. But then again, the right roommate gets most of their work done deep in The Stacks, where people only seem to go to find forgotten books, or cry, or fuck, so maybe it's possible: different strokes, different folks. Xay's had sex in The Stacks, not with the right roommate, but before they dated, with his last partner, which the right roommate has to admit, they find a little intimidating: no judgement, just that the right room-mate could never, not in The Stacks, or in the Colcannon dining hall, or The Meditation Garden, or really anywhere that's not one of their rooms, usually the right roommate's, since Xay lives in a giant, top-floor quad, with three of his best friends, people whom the right roommate admires, and would like to know better, but is nevertheless also intimidated by, since they're all so cool, and the right roommate is the right roommate, which brings them back to the conundrum of the text, and figuring out tomorrow's plans: Xay almost certainly already has Carneval plans with his roommates, so it's just a question of how the right roommate will figure into those, and whether they'll have to invite themselves, or whether Xay will have to break off from his plans and come hang out with the right roommate and maybe the left roommate and a few of their, the roommates', friends, which it's possible, the right roommate supposes, Xay's friends would resent, fur-thering the feeling the right roommate has that they are re-sented in general by Xay's friends, a feeling that might be less-ened if Xay ever invited the right roommate to hang out with them, but that really didn't seem likely, the right roommate concludes, as they check their phone and see nothing on the screen.

As the right roommate contemplates a double text, the left roommate waits in line at The Tavern, a veritable University institution, one of only a few restaurants allowed to operate on campus. Actually, it, along with most of the others, belongs to a single owner, something you would never think, since all the restaurants seem so different, but if you really sit down to think about it, as the left roommate has, it shouldn't be surprising: scratch a vibe and see what bleeds.

It's easy to be cynical, especially for the left roommate, who's just crawled out of the throes of a particularly sophomoric disillusionment with their life and with University as a whole; it's the kind of disillusionment that lives in that space between idea and reality, the kind of place where you might realize, for instance, that your college experience has little or nothing to do with The College Experience; that out of that nebulous solution of infinite possibility has crystallized something imperfect and disappointing, something that exists, something that's yours, a reality, the precipitate of utopia; and the thing about utopian precipitates, the thing about realities, the left roommate has decided, after many rounds of afternoon discussion, is that you can't really uncrystallize them: you can change them, you can chip away the details, you can melt them down and start all over again, but you can never go back: once it's yours, it's yours. Here's an obvious profundity: you're never going to change the past. Never. Stare at it all you want, let it inform your present, let it guide your future, but don't, for a second, be delusional: it's not changing. Few things are impossible; this is.

The left roommate knows this. They're trans, after all, and the thing about them being trans, they've decided, after many, many rounds of afternoon discussion, is that there are some things that they're just never going to get: the past they want, mainly; that's gone. But at least the future's up for grabs, and, reasons the left roommate, if there are some things that you're just never going to get, you might as well demand everything else.

So yes, the left roommate isn't particularly swayed by the fake oak barrels, or the fake fireplace, or the dim lighting, or any of the other curated signifiers The Tavern has installed to give the illusion of a jovial place to drink, but as they walk through The Tavern, and outside, precariously balancing the plate of fries with one hand, and the overflowing pitcher with the other, they can't help but notice that everyone here really does seem jovial—jolly, even. There's a real happiness here, at The Tavern.

And then the left roommate looks at the right roommate, absorbed in their phone, mouthing the words of some over-thought text, and they feel sad, sad for their friend, who seems constitutionally incapable of standing up for themself. It's obvious that they're still trying to text Xay, to get what they want without seeming like they want it, and without infringing on anything that Xay wants, god forbid the right roommate get something at the expense of someone else, something the right roommate only seems capable of doing by accident. It's a little pathetic, honestly, bordering on infuriating, but they're friends, so it's mostly just sad.

— Food and beer have arrived.

— Oh, thanks, how much do I owe you?

— Don't worry about it.

— You sure?

Nodding,

— So, I've been thinking about that clown.

— What about him?

— I guess I've just been thinking that there have to be peo-ple who are really like that. People that could just disappear and no one would know.

— You think?

— Yeah. Fringe people. People that are just out there.

The right roommate pecks at some fries.

— And I guess what I've been thinking about that is that I think for a long time I wanted to be one of those people, someone at the fringe, I dunno, like just fuck off to a farm somewhere and raise goats and get away from all, — gestur-ing, — this. And I know that's way too romantic, and that even if you drop out of a broken system, you're still leaving it broken for everyone else, and it's irresponsible and immoral and if I have the privilege of coolly making these observations, then I have a responsibility to change things and blah blah blah, but like fuck, it's still kind of tempting.

— Yeah.

— But then I started thinking, it doesn't really have to be spatial. The fringe. Like it's easier to think about someone living in a shack in the woods, but you can live in a society and still be pretty fringe. Like intellectually speaking, there's a fringe. We have all of these thought systems and ideologies that are sort of mainstreamed, or not like mainstream, but I guess, institutional? Like oh if you want to know about power then you *have* to read Bouillabaisse, and if you want to know about the law then you *have* to read Calzone, and you don't even need to have read them, since their ideas have sort of like percolated through our whole society so even if you haven't read them, you've read them. Their ideas are like part of our world. They're at the core.

— Okay.

— And now think about how you engage with ideas. Imagine that your mind is like this blank slate, and every time you engage with an idea it like carves a groove in your mind and that's a path for your thoughts to go down, right? So like if you read Bouillabaisse then there's a Bouillabaisse groove in your head and whenever you think about power your thoughts go down this Bouillabaisse groove, and that like determines the direction of your thoughts. And it's pretty obvious how that works for intellectual stuff. But it also works for feelings. Like if you're gay, and you consume a bunch of homophobic media, and talk to a bunch of homophobic people, and live in a homophobic society, it carves this groove into your brain that says that gay people are worthless. And that groove is big. It's deep. So the next time something bad happens to you, your feelings are flooding through your mind and they naturally go to this big, deep groove that says that gay people are worthless, and thus you're worthless, and you should be angry at yourself. But if you do the work of digging another groove, a bigger groove, one that says that a homophobic society is worthless, then maybe the next time your feelings will go down that, and you won't be angry at yourself, you'll be angry at like society. Am I making any sense?

— Not really.

— Fuck, okay. Basically like you have all these thought slash feelings grooves in your head, right? And you share them with a ton of people since a ton of people learn the same things in school, and read the same books, and live in the same society, and whatever. But you know, depending on the various circumstances of your life, all these grooves are going to be different sizes, and, AND, much more importantly, they're going to be connected in different ways. When you do your own thinking, it's really about connecting the grooves. Synthesizing all the things you've learned. So sometimes things dig the grooves for you, sometimes you dig them yourself. It goes both ways. Is *that* making any sense?

— It's really not.

— Okay well this probably won't help, but I was reading about this thing called a connectome, which is basically like a map of all the neural connections in your brain. Like a neural fingerprint. That's what it's like physically. But like abstractly, if you think about it in terms of the grooves I've been describing, we're all unique thinkers because we have this unique system of grooves for our thoughts and feelings to go through. But again, a lot of us have similar groove maps because we read the same books, and watch the same TV, and live in the same society, and so on. And all that makes it pretty easy to see where most other people's thoughts are coming from. Like you're talking to someone about like movies and they're talking about like the 'hollowness of industriality' and you're thinking, oh okay this dude is a total Spätzle-head, but then, *then* you meet people that are really out there. Conspiracy theorist maybe, or cult member, or just like, really trippy people. And you're talking to them and you have no idea what sort of grooves their thoughts are running through because they're operating on like totally different planes of thought. They're fringe thinkers.

— Right.

— And you know, like, what if they're right?

— About what?

— I dunno, everything! What if some trippy crank's figured out all the secrets to the universe and we're out here reading Bouillabaisse like a bunch of fucking idiots?

— . . .

— . . .

— . . .

— Basically I'm saying I think we should start doing more Drugs.

— That's funny.

— What?

— I was just thinking the opposite.

— Yeah?

— Yeah. I just . . . I don't think smoking weed is good for me.

— What do you mean?

— It's just . . . it's not good. For me.

— Why not?

— I don't think I can do a good job of explaining it.

— Tryyyyy.

The right roommate tactically sips their beer. But they can only sip their beer for so long.

— It's just not fun anymore. Every time I get high I'm just . . . stressed.

— But everything stresses you out.

— Exactly! So why make it worse?

— . . .

— Like I've been trying to text Xay for literally hours and I can't because every time I think of something to say it explodes into like a million different things that Xay thinks I could be saying and then each of those explodes into like a million different things and on and on and on and it's so fucking exhausting. And like every time I think that smoking weed is going to make things better, things just get worse. Maybe my head's just fucked up. I don't know. I'm sorry.

The left roommate downs the rest of their beer. They look around. Everyone still seems jovial. Things still feel real. They look at the right roommate checking their phone.

— But you think the problem is weed?

— Don't tell me it's my thought grooves.

— I mean yes, but, — says the left roommate, seeing their window and hurtling through, — no. I think the real problem is Xay.

— What?

— He treats you like shit, dude! Like I don't know any other way to say it but it's not normal. — Perceiving. — I'm sorry, I really am, but I've been waiting too long to say this. You should not be afraid of your boyfriend. And you are! Like every time you're with him it feels like you're walking on eggshells like he's this fucking powder keg that's going to explode if you say the wrong thing and it's not good; it's really fucking unhealthy.

— I'm not afraid of him.

— You are though. You really are.

— I'm intimidated by him.

— How is that not the same?

— Because it's not like I'm . . . scared of him. I just, you know, he's so cool and beautiful and smart and like sure of himself, and I'm like me, you know. So of course I'm intimidated by him. But that's just . . . I mean . . . what do you want me to say? That I think he's better than me? Of course I think he's better than me. Why would I date someone I thought was worse?

— You really think he's better than you?

— You really don't?

— Of course not. Just because he's skinny and white and rich-

— I'm skinny and white and rich.

— He just sucks. I'm sorry. I don't know any other way to say it. He sucks. And his friends suck. And their friends suck. And I just feel like someone needs to say it and none of our friends will. But it sucks. It sucks watching you shrink yourself to be with this person that doesn't even fucking care about you.

— How do you know that he doesn't care about me?

— Because I see you, R., I see the way he talks to you and I see the way you are around him.

— You don't see us when we're alone.

— I shouldn't have to.

R. looks into their beer. They don't want to be here anymore. Maybe Xay is right. Maybe the left roommate is domineering and bitter and wanting to break up R. and Xay because they resent how much time R. spends with him; maybe the left roommate *is* jealous . . . and were they mad that R. wanted to stop smoking weed? Xay thinks that they, the roommates, don't really have anything in common besides the fact that they like to get high, and watch TV, and argue about bullshit; that this isn't a good foundation for a relationship; that the left roommate is taking advantage of R. because they don't have very many other friends, and because R.—let's face it—lets people walk all over them; that R. is better than the left roommate; that they should reassign into a co-op, where they'd have more of a community and be happier.

But R. likes arguing about bullshit and watching TV and getting high with the left roommate.

And they like Xay.

God.

— I'm too high to have this conversation.

— Fine.

Maybe they should break up with Xay.

— . . .

Maybe they should reassign.

— . . .

Maybe they should break up with Xay and reassign.

— . . .

They check their phone.

— . . .

They'll stop smoking weed, at least.
— …
For a week.
— …
See how it goes.
— …
But tomorrow's Carneval.
— …
Starting Sunday then.
— …
Monday, start of the week.
— …
They check their phone.
— …
Maybe.
— I …
— Yes?
No. Not worth it.
— I'm going to go to the bathroom, — says R.
— Okay.
— I'm not mad, R.
— Okay.

R. gets up from the table, walks past the conspiratorial grad students (now dispersing), past the loud boys (still discoursing), and into The Tavern, where they make a beeline for the bathroom. The other R. sits at the table and watches as Mike Beef and a few of the other Weekly editors walk into The Tavern to spend their free meal credit on nachos and beer.

It's beautiful outside, like everything's suspended in amber. But nothing's really suspended in amber. Nothing real. Time's still time. Always moving.

5:53 PM

Over the wall dividing two showers:

— You're peeing.

— …

— You're doing it on the drain, which is considerate, but it's a different stream, different sound, one can tell.

— …

— It's not that I care, I just thought that maybe you'd like to know.

It stops.

— Wonderful!

— What's your problem?

— How long do you have?

Nothing.

— Well, I'm glad you got it all out, I would've felt bad if you'd stopped half way through. That's a terrible feeling, starting and stopping like that. Once, when-

— Do you do this a lot?

— Me? Never, I go before.

— …

— No, you're my first I'm afraid, once I was pure!

— . . .

The sounds of water hitting bodies.

— You asked me what my problem is?

— . . .

— What makes you so sure I have one? Is this not what one would call normal behavior?

— . . .

— You're the shower pee-er.

— . . .

— I suppose my problem is I want to leave.

— The curtain's unlocked.

Guffaws.

Nothing.

— Query: when you pee in the shower, do you think about whether others can hear you? Or smell, I suppose, but I noticed you were washing at the same time, which was crafty . . . very crafty.

— . . .

— Do you condition?

— . . .

— You must. You sound like a man who cares about his hair.

— . . .

— How do you wear it?

— . . .

— Tell me something about yourself, mystery man.

— . . .

— Or perhaps you'd like to hear something about moi . . . ?

— . . .

— Hmm.

— . . .

A bottle is placed on the shower floor.

— Don't you feel, I don't know, rather judged?

— . . .

— When you pee, I mean.

— . . .

— Anyone would, which must mean you don't care. Don't such things trouble you? People knowing you're a shower pee-er and all that.

— . . .

— But would they even . . . I see! How would they know who you are? What anonymity the shower curtain doth bring!

— . . .

— Hmm, but then you can't step out of the shower until they've left entirely. You must take quite long showers.

— . . .

— You do know we're still in a drought?

— . . .

— Well, my friend, you've convinced me!

The sounds, and smell, of urine hitting a shower drain.

— Do you always have such a weak stream?

— Oh, only when I'm erect.

— . . .

— That was a joke.

— . . .

— You didn't laugh.

— It wasn't funny.

— You know, you're very to the point. I like that; it's charming.

— …

— So what is it you plan to do when you leave this shower?

— …

— Dining hall?

— …

— No, no need to shower before that . . . might one be going on a date?

— …

— Of course . . . and who is this lucky soul?

— …

— A lover, I presume?

— …

— How long have you been dating?

— …

— Do you love her?

— …

— Or him? Them?

— Her.

— Ah, you must. Have you told her?

A pause.

— You're single.

— Alas! I am, thank you for asking.

— I wasn't.

— …

— …

— And from whence did you come?

— 'Whence.'

— Yes.

— Are you a theater kid?

— What?

— The way you talk.

— What of it?

— Yeah, that. It's affected right, this gentleman-dandy thing you're doing?

— I must say I have no idea wh-

— You do, cut the shit. People don't talk that way. Is it part of a bit?

— . . .

— Is it so I don't know who you are?

— No.

— What then?

— . . .

— You were so talkative before.

— . . .

— Is this going the way you'd pictured it?

— . . .

— Yeah, I didn't think so.

It's just the sounds of the shower. A minute passes.

— The gym.

— What?

— The gym is from whence I came.

A laugh.

— You lift?

— . . .

— . . .

More silence.

— So you want to drop out?

— What?

— You said your problem was that you wanted to leave.
You want to leave University?

— I guess.

— . . .

— Leave everything.

— . . .

— . . .

— You want to kill yourself?

An appropriate amount of time passes.

— No.

— Then?

— I don't know.

— . . .

— . . .

— You know, I think I liked the gentleman-dandy thing
more. You should go back to that.

— . . .

— So this is, what, a cry for help?

— More of an experiment.

— Testing what?

— . . .

— . . .

— I wanted to see if I could feel like someone else.

— Did it work?

Snort.

— Guess not.

— . . .

The door to the bathroom opens. Footsteps move from the door to the sink, pause, and then into the stall. A few seconds later, a stream opens up against the inside of a porcelain bowl, followed by a short grunt, a second, and then, like a diver sliding seamlessly into a pool, a small splash.

— So, what are we discussing today, boys?

— . . .

— . . .

— Aww, the boys are bashful. No need. We could all hear you from the courtyard.

— Go fuck yourself.

— Easy there, no need for any vulgarities. If you two want a moment together, far be it from me to intrude. I'll just finish up here and get on with my day.

— . . .

— . . .

— You know what I think, though?

— . . .

— . . .

— And granted I could only make out bits and pieces of what y'all were talking about, but I think y'all *were* having a moment.

— . . .

— . . .

— Pretty cute.

— What the fuck do you want?

— Me? I am strictly here for observational purposes. It's not every day that you get to witness a shower conversation in the flesh.

— . . .

— . . .

— And I'm sorry to share this with you gentlemen, but we seem to have encountered some gridlock here; that is, despite being in session, congress is now refusing to pass legislation, which is to say y'all are unfortunately stuck with me, at least for the duration of your shower, I'd expect, so . . . might as well fire it back up, boys.

— . . .

— Do you think people really change?

— Don't indulge him.

— It doesn't matter. He already heard us.

— Indeed. Do I think people really change? Of course. Everything changes. People grow.

— Some decay.

— Somber fella, ain't ya?

— You too? Fuck me, is it bit day?

— Pardon?

— Exactly.

— But it's all a performance, right? One can speak like this, and say such marvelous things, but at the end of the day, even if I talk like this, I'm still performing. For you. For the constipated cowboy. For whoever. We all have ideas about the kind of person we want to be, and we try to be that person. But we never will be. That person doesn't exist. They're just an idea. Ideas are coherent. People aren't. That's why people don't want people. Your boss doesn't want a person. They want a worker. Your girlfriend doesn't want a person. She wants a lover. Your professor doesn't want a person. They want a student. And that's why we're always having to be different people all the time, because nobody wants us, they just want a function. Maybe that's too cynical. I don't know. I don't think it's a bad thing. I just think it's a thing. When you're doing something the action changes you. You become someone else. And then when you're done you revert back to baseline. The real you. The you that's not doing anything. The you that's just existing. My problem is that I hate that me. If I'm doing something, or being someone for somebody, then I'm fine. But when I'm alone. When I'm just existing. It's empty. I don't see the point. So that's what I mean when I say that I want to leave. It's this feeling I get, like I always have to be somewhere else. To be someone else. I don't think that's normal. I think most people are fine being themselves. So I don't know why I'm not. I don't think I'm special. I think I'm fucked up. Something's wrong with me. But I also think I'm right. About people. I think you think you're a consistent person because you talk normal, and you work out, and you have a girlfriend, and I bet you make good grades and get good internships and get along with your parents, but I think you change. I think you think you're above that, but you're not. No one is.

— God. You are a theater kid.

— Fuck you! I'm serious.

After a pause,

— Yes. Of course I change. But I am normal. I do get good grades. I do work out. I do have a girlfriend. I have problems, too. I'm complex. But I'm normal. I'm not like you. You need me to be normal because it validates your abnormality. You do think you're special. But you're not. You're just fucked up. You give dramatic speeches to people who are showering next to you instead of going to therapy like you should. Nobody just exists. I'm normal because I do the work. Because I understand that being a person is work. You know, I take it back: I think deep down you don't think that normal people exist, that they can't exist, that everyone is secretly like you. You think that because it gives you an excuse to do nothing about it. But there's no excuse. I work to be normal. Everyone does.

Clapping his hands together,

— Oooh-ee, boys! This is what I came for.

— I don't think everyone does. I think there are plenty of people who are normal because they don't think about any of this.

Scoffs,

— What, you think you need a University degree to get existential? Fuck you're clueless. Are you a freshman?

A pause,

— So?

Laughing,

— Of course you are. Talk to me in three years.

The door to the bathroom opens again.

— Jedidiah, brother, you in here?

— Right here, partner. Hope y'all don't mind I invited a friend.

— Brought Enrique and Joey with me, too.

— Hey.   — Yo.

— We were just discussing normality, and the pursuit of a better life. Feel free to resume, boys.

— Fuck you.

— Why don't we ask them? Enrique, Joey do you think you're normal?

— Hell yeah!   — Hell no!

— Actually, bro?

— I know my worth.

— Jedidiah?

— I reckon ... I reckon that this here construction of normality, like most others, is a violent project of personhood imposed by the ruling class on their inferiors as a means of social control. To the point that our own project of a personhood is an ongoing struggle with the self, I am largely in agreement. However, I would caution our aggrieved showerer that such a view elides the systemic nature of our unfortunate young man's struggle to find himself. And I would suggest to him that he ought to see the struggle with the self, not as a solitary project, but a social one: a struggle against the various selves that society has imposed on our unfortunate young man in the form of functions, something which he has so keenly identified, on today, Friday, the day before Carneval.

— Damn.   — Damn.

— I'm just fuckin around. Course I feel normal. Doesn't everyone?

— Before today I would've said that nobody does.

— Some people do. Some people don't. It's not that complicated. You're overthinking it.

— ...

— . . .   — . . .

— . . .

— Say more about this systemic thing.

— Or don't.

— You think it's all individual?

— Of course not. Of course it's systemic. Of course it's so-cietal. But that doesn't mean you don't have to do the work. Look: you're fucked up. That much is clear. But the last thing you need right now is for someone to tell you that this is some-one else's fault. It doesn't matter whose fault it is. It's your problem. Nobody's going to solve it for you. Not me. Not Enrique. Not Joey. Not Jedidiah. Not your friends. Not your therapist. Not the government. You. You have to do the work. You have to do the work today, you have to do the work to-morrow, you have to do the work every day until you die.

— Damn.   —Damn.

— He needs to hear it. That's what life is. Work. You don't like being yourself? Change yourself.

— But I have! Even since coming here I'm a totally dif-ferent person. I like different things. I have different friends. My politics are different. My interests are different. I cut my hair. I've changed. And I still feel this like wrongness. Like ev-ery version of myself is wrong. Like as soon as I become aware that I'm a type, like the type of guy who likes X, the type of guy who says Y, the type of guy who believes in Z, then I can't stand it anymore. I have to be something different. So I'm al-ways changing who I am. But I'm also never changing. I'm still myself. I'm still fucked up.

— So take some time off. Go home. Work. Hang out with

your parents. Read. Exercise. See a therapist. Do the work. Then come back.

— I guess.

— . . .

— Fuck this.   — I'm out.

— Peace.

Two pairs of feet on the move. The door opens and closes.

— What if that doesn't work? What if I take some time off and I go home and I work a job and I hang out with my parents and read and exercise and see a therapist, and after all that, I'm just stuck there feeling like the guy who took time off and went home and read and exercised and saw a therapist, and I still hate it?

— Then you try something else.

— But what?

— Figure it out yourself, fuck.

— Sorry I-

— If I may interject, — says Jedidiah, — do you have friends?

— What?

— Friends. Do you have them?

— Yes.

— And they like you?

— As far as I know.

— Significant other?

— Not interested.

— And your grades?

— They're fine.

— Do you have a job?

— I'm a Cobbler Scholar.

— A Cobbler Scholar! Well I'll be damned. So here we have a nice, University boy, a boy with friends, with good grades, a Cobbler Scholar, in fact. A boy with all the markers of success, and yet he hates who he is.

— So we've figured out that success doesn't make you happy. Go us.

— A banal observation, no doubt. However, what I'm proposing to our little symposium here is that we consider the converse. For does it not seem that it's precisely your, shall we call it, condition, your fear of being a type, that has driven you to continually refine yourself into a more successful, more bespoke individual? Do you not feel bespoke?

— I feel fucked up.

— Why are you encouraging him? He doesn't need to feel special; he needs to-

— 'Do the work,' I agree. But look here: you want to change.

— Yes.

— You want to be different.

— Yes.

— You're sick of the struggle.

— Yes!

— But can you let go?

— What?

— What, my friend, are you willing to lose?

— I still don't understand.

Jedidiah flushes.

— You will. Now then, boys, I believe I'll be taking my leave. Ali, shall we?

— Yeah, I'm coming.

The door to the stall opens; the sink runs, stops. Jedidiah and Ali leave.

— What did he mean?

— He's just fucking with you.

— . . .

— . . .

— . . .

— So are you going to drop out?

— I don't know.

— Yeah.

— . . .

— . . .

— Call MENTAL. Tell them you want to hurt yourself, otherwise it'll be months before you see anyone.

— Okay.

— Tell the therapist what you told me.

— Okay.

— And never do this again.

— Okay.

— . . .

— Are you going to talk about this?

— . . .

— On the date?

— . . .

— I'm sure you will.

— Don't be.

Then the water's off. The curtain's moved. The sink's on, and the room is filled with the soothing hum of an electric toothbrush. The sink's off. A comb runs through hair. A hint of cologne. The sink's on again, and over the noise of the running shower, and the sink, just barely, you can hear the sound of a razor gliding across flesh. Then the sink's off again. The bathroom door opens, holds for a second, and closes. The shower runs.

Night

Dinner happened; now Ana Turrón is in the shower, thinking about her problems. She's got a few, computer stuff, mostly: her coursework, a personal project or two, some hangups from last summer's work. Right now she's thinking about something from class, an unproven optimality conjecture and a self-adjusting tree, but there's a reason it's stayed unproven, and Ana, feeling her mind slipping, decides to give it a rest.

This is nice. Hot water on her skin, nothing in her head.

But it can't last: she's a thinker, Ana Turrón, and as her brain fires back up, it's only natural she thinks about tonight's plans, all but opening up the curtain and inviting in the rest of her problems—the human stuff—which, sure enough, have already sent their main stooge, what in University shorthand goes by The Demon: the sort of indeterminate, scale-dropping, slime-dripping *thing* that slithers up your leg, wraps itself around your torso, and, as you look for something sharp to swing, puts its head close to yours, tongues your ear a little, and says: it's time to flake.

Speed dating and the drag show. These are Ana's big plans. But now that The Demon's making its case, she's not so sure.

What you need, what you want, it says, is to log on to Da.te and withdraw from tonight's pool, to text Mari and say that you're not really feeling up to going out tonight, that it's been a long week (it had), that you have stuff to do (she did), and that you'll be staying home (she could). Yes, The New Plan, as it stands, oozing out The Demon's mouth, is to put on a movie she's seen before, get kind of drunk, and epilate—what, it assures her, she's been feeling she needs to do all week.

She looks down. True, she thinks, tonight could be productively spent ripping all the hair out of her legs; it's also true that doing so might put out some of the mild dysphoria she's feeling now, looking at her legs, instead of the alternative, feeding it with gasoline, the inevitable consequence of her current plans—but it's also also true that Ana has goals tonight, inevitable consequence-wise, so, grabbing The Demon by the throat, and giving it a good squeeze, she decides: speed dating and the drag show.

A few minutes later Ana Turrón sits at her desk, spinning slightly in her chair, naked, her eyes glazed and up at the tapestry stretched across her ceiling, her legs splayed out, her stomach still digesting, her fingers doing a little earring-fiddling—would she need to dress up? Not for the speed dating. It's a tech event, and even amongst her heather-hoodied peers, Ana Turrón is a more committed sartorial insurgent than most. No, it's tonight's second event that poses the real question, an opportunity to see and be seen, to venture outside her usual repertoire and go for something bold. She stands up and turns to face the large mirror propped up against the wall behind her desk. Or maybe not.

As she goes to find a top, her phone buzzes. Maybe it's her ex.

But it's just Jess.

Jess Zeppole: hi hello hi

Jess Zeppole: did you hear about this thing in Main Quad?

Ana Turrón: Saw the email but didn't open it

Jess Zeppole: apparently someone killed themself

Jess Zeppole: like with fire

Ana grabs a sweater as the she's-still-typing ellipsis floats on her screen.

Jess Zeppole: you want the video?

Ana Turrón: Holy shit, when??

Ana Turrón: No I'll pass on the video, thx

Jess Zeppole: way before anyone got up apparently so no one saw it but the video looks pretty real

Ana Turrón: Wow

Now it's Jess' turn to wait patiently for the next text.

Ana Turrón: Actually, can you send that video?

Jess Zeppole: yeah lemme find a link that works

One click, thirteen seconds, and a keyboard shortcut later, Ana Turrón is up to speed.

Ana Turrón: I don't know, looks fake to me. Last summer I was on this team that was doing stuff with video generation and something like this wouldn't be impossible to fake

Jess Zeppole: mmmmmm

Jess Zeppole: but why

Ana Turrón: Idk

Jess Zeppole: same

A minute passes.

Jess Zeppole: when's your thing?

Ana Turrón: In an hour

Jess Zeppole: mmmm

Jess Zeppole: lmao have i sent you this

Jess sends a good meme. After a couple seconds deciding how to laugh, Ana settles on:

Ana Turrón: lmao

The conversation fizzles out. Ana Turrón's alone again.

☐

At exactly 7:30 PM, Ana opens her computer, removes the piece of tape covering the camera, and logs onto Da.te.

The conceit of Da.te is fairly straightforward: over the course of the allotted event time, members of a group are paired up for two-and-a-half-minute sessions using Da.te's patented, crystal-clear, no-loss, no-lag video chat; at the end of the 'da.te,' participants are given exactly thirty seconds to decompress and rank their 'da.te-e,' one star to five. Da.te then learns using the data from each subsequent round to further refine its matching algorithm, constructing what Da.te engineers tell their business reps is called a compatibility matrix. Exactly ten rounds occur and at the end of the half hour, users are given a list of their matches' profiles and the option to share any relevant contact information. Users are also given the option of ending the chat at any time during the two-and-a-half-minute session.

The overwhelming majority of Ana's da.tes end with the use of this feature. Tonight, three did not.

(da.te 2)

Pretty eyes and overdressed:

— Josh.

— Hi, Ana.

— Alright, Ana, — he says, clapping his hands together, — I have a confession.

— Um-

— I'm not a coder.

— Sorry?

— Can't code, engineer, problem-solve; if Math is involved, basically, then I'm out. I know this is supposed to be a thing for 'techies' or whatever, and myself being a — here really going all in on the scare quotes — 'fuzzy' and all, I figured I'd be upfront about it, you know, if that's not what you're looking for, then go ahead and eject right on out of here.

— You know, I'm a very accepting person, Josh.

— Oh, fabulous! You're a techie I take it?

— Yep. Are you at University or . . . ?

— Oh no no no, I'm in the industry.

— Ah cool, are you like a tech writer?

— Right now I'm a, — straightening himself up and puffing out his chest, — Picture Guy.

— 'Picture Guy'?

— Yeah so basically what I've been doing for the past month is going through all the reported profile pictures and tagging them so the algorithms can learn to recognize whatever our fine, rebellious youth have decided is sufficiently edgy. So day-to-day, I mostly just look at infected assholes, which is what's uh 'in' right now, in case you were wondering.

— Wow . . . infected assholes, that sounds . . . fun. But isn't that kind of, I don't know, inefficient?

Grabbing his heart,

— Ana! You're killing me!

— Sorry, sorry, I didn't mean-

— I'm kidding, don't worry, yeah I honestly have no idea why they haven't fired me yet. I mean before I was a Picture Guy they had me doing all sorts of crazy shit. I was the of-ficial company Trip Sitter for a while, that was wild, but uh don't tell anyone about that one it's supposed to be a secret, and hmm well yeah now that I think about it I guess I'm also the company Drug Dealer? Which you might also want to keep under wraps. Hmm. Coffee runs. Some HR stuff. The occasional murder. Guess I'm just the all-purpose, in-house Goon.

Laughing,

— Should you be telling me all this?

— I honestly don't know. No? Let's go with no. I mean I probably shouldn't be talking ever, if we're being honest, but you're very pretty, so I'm a little nervous.

Ana blushes and the 10 second timer flashes.

— And we're running out of time! Fuck! Okay look I'm going to send you my number, if you want effusive compan-ionship or Tr-Y or something PLEASE hit me up, I'm sorry I took up-

But the session's already over.

Ana gives him four stars.

(da.te 4)

Scruffy beard, boyish face, quick with the formalities:

— Damn so you're into the real like metal stuff? — he asks.

— I mean I'm not locked into anything but yeah lately I've been kind of interested in computer architecture-

— Word, yeah. — Running a hand through his hair, — man I feel like architecture like as a like *concept* just explains so much shit.

— What do you mean?

— Like. Okay, so here's my thing, right? Like when you're starting out your project you're pretty much just rigging up something functional because you just gotta get some shit out there that works, right?

— Sure.

— And then once it's working you start just building all the other shit on top of it and when that shit's working like I don't know how often are people really just overhauling their like architecture or whatever, you know, like that's the core shit, so here you are like two years later trying to keep this giant thing afloat on all this shitty old code and nothing is working and all you can do is a bunch of these hotfixes because any real change is going to mean digging into the architecture of the whole thing, and if you're going to do that your shit's gotta go down, like it's just gotta go down and if you can't afford to do that then there's just no way like just no fucking way to fix anything. And that's basically true for everything when you get down to it right, it's pretty much all about scale and if your shit doesn't *scale* then what the fuck, you know?

Ana laughs,

— Yeah, I mean that's not exactly the kind of architecture I'm talking about but I know what you mean. When I was interning at Feed we had to do that. Rebuild the whole thing from scratch. It was such a pain, we spent the whole summer trying to build this . . . okay well I can't really talk about it but by the end of it I just wanted to run off a cliff.

He nods, a couple seconds pass. He looks concerned.

— I mean okay it wasn't actually that bad-

— No for sure . . . for sure.

Unsure of what to do, she fakes a cough. Neither says anything for a couple of seconds. She moves her mouse over the eject button, but the timer's basically run out.

Two stars.

(da.te 10)

Older-looking, visible signs of distress—hold on, doesn't she . . .

— Is it . . . erm . . . Anna?

— Ana, yeah . . . sorry, I recognize you but I can't remember . . . were you at eXe?

He nods.

— John Mung. I believe we met at the End of Summer Boat Party.

— Right! Right, okay, now I remember. OH, — she says, audibly intrigued, — you work in Building C.

— Yes.

— Still not taking interns?

— I'm afraid not.

— Bummer.

— Of course, a coder of your erm prowess would be very welcome but Building C requires a certain fidelity that an intern cannot-.

— You're the AGI guy!

— Pardon?

— Sorry, didn't mean to cut you off, I just remembered, you were telling me about the like what was it cascading recursive something?

— Recursive Cascade Correlation, yes it's-

— RIGHT, wild. Sorry, go ahead.

— I was only going to say that we've in fact been using some of the code you worked on last summer, what you did with those GANs, it's . . . quite remarkable.

— Thank you, wow, I can't believe . . . but what would you . . . y'all wouldn't have happened to have made a video of someone on fire would you?

He looks confused.

— Someone on fire?

— There's this video . . . actually, never mind, I'm sure you wouldn't be able to tell me what you're doing anyways.

— By no choice of my own.

— Mmm yeah you say the wrong thing and one of those eXe drones is going to come and . . . — seeing John Mung's look of horror — or you know . . .

— Yes. The NDA.

A brief silence.

— Perhaps . . . coffee?

— Uh yeah, sure, here, — she says, checking her calendar — I've got some time next week.

— Wonderful.

In the time they have left, they settle on a date. The session runs out. Ana gives John four stars, sends him her contact info, and closes the app.

She stretches in her chair, looking at the sliver of window not covered by the curtain, wondering what someone walking by could see.

She looks down. There are a pair of wristbands she needs somewhere on her desk. Mari'll be over in half an hour, she should get ready.

□

— He seemed weird? Keep your head . . . yes perfect.

— Not weird, just like off? I don't know, he was nice. And I mean, — pausing, — he does AGI, — she says, sexually.

— Ana . . .

Ana giggles to herself.

— You've got a problem you know.

— Don't kinkshame me.

— Me? — says Mari, pulling just a little too tight, — your hair is so soft.

— I wish I could cut it.

— Really?

— Yeah, I mean I like it, it's just a pain. I don't know, maybe in a year.

— Do you have a — Ana holds up a hair tie — perfect

okay . . . done! Hmm. Yes. They're fabulous, what can I say? I'm an artiste.

Ana looks in the mirror, seeing the braids and feeling, as she still does, that little rush of recognition—but seeing herself is here cut short by the sudden, unwelcome entrance of her hairline, really the corners of her hairline, which sit way back on her head, like someone pulled them back and never let go.

— You're an artiste! — Ana says, grabbing one of the beanies scattered around her desk, — without you I'd be-

— Hopeless, yes exactly what I was thinking, — says Mari, grabbing the beanie out of Ana's hand and tossing it back on her desk.

— Hmm . . . — now it's Mari's turn to look in the mirror. In honor of the occasion, she's gone for slicked-back hair, a white shirt, a leather jacket, a pair of painted-on sideburns, and boots. — Do I need something else?

— You're perfect. You think a lot of people'll come in drag?

Still looking in the mirror, Mari pulls out a cigarette and growls a little. She turns to Ana.

— 'Come serving a look,' it said. Does this count? Are looks being served?

— All the looks.

Mari looks Ana up and down. Ana's wearing black joggers and an oversized hoodie.

— But what sort of looks is Ana serving tonight, hmm?

Ana looks at Mari.

Mari looks at Ana.

— Ummmmmmmm, — says Ana, laying it on a little thick, — this is a *man's* hoodie? There's this thing called Subtle Drag.

— No there isn't.

Hands in the air and really just going for it now,

— Oh so now you're going to cisplain drag to a . . . hey!

Her eyes rolled dangerously far back into her head, Mari had nevertheless managed to flick her cigarette with laser precision right at Ana's nose, which it hit, bouncing off and falling somewhere on the floor. Ana looks at it longingly before picking it up and handing it back to Mari.

— Should we go?

— We, — says Mari, checking her phone, — should go.

The two exit Ana's room, Ana complaining about not being able to smoke, Mari making sympathetic noises as she responds to some texts, both unconsciously bracing themselves for the night chill.

Almost nine, a strange time for these University streets: nay a jogger in sight, and only a few bikers, most having already gone home, or not planning to; it's early still for those roaming packs of freshman, always loud, usually lost, led, every now and then, by that leader-type who breaks off from the pack and goes a few steps ahead, walking backwards and confidently reassuring the rest of the crew that they know where they're going, that there is in fact a party there, that if they just turn left here and then definitely a right up ahead . . . eventually slipping back into the anonymity of that fluid drunken braid, bodies matching words as they weave in and out, missing, colliding, yelping; there are a couple cars out too; a cop, maybe; some squirrels; the moon; our two girls, a little red dot floating alongside them.

Their talk fills the streets. Mari has been recounting to Ana some of the research she's been doing for her thesis—prions are involved, and Ana's ashamed to admit that despite these weekly updates from her close friend, she still hasn't managed to get a hang of the bio babble, the -pathies and -ases, the mechanisms and molecules, all daisy-chained together by phrases Ana's pretty sure she knows but in practice tell her nothing besides the fact that they're still speaking a language she nominally understands. An animated Mari is somewhere in the middle of a mouse vivisection when the co-op appears, vivisection turning into full-blown muricide by the time the two climb the steps and reach the front door, flashing their wristbands at the couple working security, reading the sign out loud ('Consent is a verbal affirmation . . . '), and entering, at last, into the house's grungy interior.

— The show's in the lounge?

— It starts there. It's one of those . . . — but Mari trails off, momentarily stunned by the sheer number of people in the lounge.

It's packed. Ana notices a fire marshal's warning posted somewhere near the lights: maximum occupancy, 89. It's been greatly exceeded. She wonders briefly how they calculate these things, looking it up on her phone so she can read up after the show.

It's one of those new shows was what Mari was going to say, the interactive kind where performers spread throughout the house and all perform their acts simultaneously, viewers scattered between them, moving rooms at the end of each act, something Ana might have thoughts about if she wasn't busy getting clocked by the sandy-haired frat boy standing a few feet in front of Mari, who's been staring at Ana intently, like there's something he needs to figure out before he can look away—which, at least, he has the good sense to do when she looks back with appropriate ice, quietly returning himself to his conversation, saying nothing, thinking god knows what. Ana checks her initial annoyance with the acknowledged possibility that yes, maybe he was also trans, or an egg, or somewhere in between, staring at Ana because he was using her to figure out what he wanted to be, whether he wanted to be like her, or be like her but Not Like *Her*, which was still weird, yeah, but obviously Ana's in no position to talk—that tall, broad-shouldered brunette's just caught her lingering, and now it's Ana turn to look away sheepishly and think, for a minute, about how she's always doing this: clocking everyone: cis women, cis men, trans women, trans men, n-bs, always comparing hip proportions and shoe sizes and jawlines, decomposing the problem into all its component parts: the feet, the hands, the shoulders, the heights, the curves, the face, the hair, what passed, what didn't, what she would keep, what she would change, as if all it took were careful study and sheer force of longing, and she could escape the body she had and fall into the one she wanted, all without having to laser off any hair or take any hormones or pay someone to cut her up and put her back together.

— Quite white in here, no? — asks Mari.

Ana looks around,

— Yeah, — and then, gesturing to herself, — same.

Mari smirks, saying nothing. Ana considers saying something else, but decides to resume her survey of the room, doing her best not to stare.

After a minute or two, the lights go down and two fabulously dressed women enter the lounge. It's the hosts, two sophomores Ana's heard of but doesn't know, one cis, one trans, both looking strong, both holding megaphones and shouting over each other, trying to explain the rules of the show: no booing, no touching, don't be a dick. Simple enough, Ana thinks.

— So without further ado, welcome to The Unholy . . .

— Glitoris!   — Chesticles!

The hosts exchange a look of exaggerated surprise.

— Glitoris! — says the one.

— Chesticles! — says the other.

— Glitoris!

— Chesticles!

— Glitoris!

— Chesticles!

Sure she's not getting it, and that whatever it was, it would keep happening until everyone had left the room, Ana grabs Mari by the arm and leads her out of the lounge and into a hallway full of people. Mari looks at her, smiling.

— I thought they looked good, no?

— The hosts?

— Yeah.

Someone from behind bumps up against her.

— Ah my b . . . what was I saying . . . right, but isn't that like hella problematic?

Ana resists the urge to turn around.

— Yeah?

— Bet. Like if they're going to set up this like genital dialectic-

From even further back, a third voice chimes,

— But I think they were being facetious.

— Yeah?

— Yeah . . . I mean right? Like it had to be a tongue-in-cheek thing.

Ana leans over and whispers to Mari.

— ¿Escuchas esto?

— No, ¿qué pasa?

But before Ana can explain, they're shuffled into the first room of the night. It's a small crowd, maybe fifteen people. Ana and Mari are in the back, Mari struggling to see, Ana fine, her eyes now trained on the pair of expansive, pink booty shorts swaying from side to side in front of her. The music starts playing and the swaying gets a little more violent, the crowd's started hooting and hollering and the music's really going now; the performer's turned around and she's wearing one of those gray University bookstore sweaters, a gigantic blonde wig, makeup Ana can't begin to make sense of, what looked like a pair of horn-rimmed glasses that had done three points of molly, a coarse brown beard, and 4.5" heels—also pink. She turns away from the crowd again, pausing as the music builds.

At the drop, she turns back again, this time with a dental dam held over her mouth. Her tongue starts thrashing. More cheers. She walks slowly toward the crowd, locking eyes with the sandy-haired frat boy, who looks somewhere between pet-rified and actually just dead—Ana's glad she's not in the first row.

And glad she's here, she decides. It's nice, seeing her feel hot.

The show finishes. It's packed in the hall. As Ana waits on the stairs, underneath a large mural of one of her favorite rappers, she listens to the people walking by:

— . . . you think they ever slip in the heels . . .

— . . . just email him and tell him you're sick or dead or something . . .

— . . . man I'm not saying it's wack because she's *naked*, I'm saying it's wack because *she's* . . .

— . . . and I still have like three different psets to do . . .

— . . . serving LOOKS, — says an excited-looking boy, throwing Mari what appears to be a high five, which she returns with force as Ana checks her phone.

John Mung: Hi Ana, this is John Mung. Can we meet tonight?

John Mung: I have to see you.

She shows Mari the phone.

— This is the guy, from earlier.

— The awkward one?

— Yeah.

Mari whistles.

— This is exciting!

— What?

— He wants to come over and talk AI . . . — she says, her eyebrows doing a little jig.

But Ana's not having it. She jams the phone back into her pocket.

— Ana, he likes you!

— I don't think so.

Mari looks at her like she's stupid, a look which Ana returns.

— He just wants to fuck a tranny, Mari.

Someone walking by looks up.

— But how can you say that!? You barely even know him!

— Exactly.

— Ana . . .

— Trust me.

Now it's Mari's turn to not be having it.

— But you said he was nice!

— So?

— So he was nice . . .

But the line on the stairs is moving. Ana and Mari enter the next room, where they're the third and fourth spectators to arrive, the rest quickly filing in behind them, leaving Ana in the front of the crowd, right square in the danger zone. She resolves not to make eye contact with the thonged but nevertheless essentially naked boy in front of her, or with the girl he's sitting on, who's leaning back in an office chair, her face obscured, her long, flowing hair, well, flowing over the mesh back of the chair, her left hand snaking around her co-performer's chest, feeling for a nipple, closing in . . . tweaking, gingerly.

The boy drops the rose from his mouth and now it's on the ground and the music's starting; he's managed to turn his body 180 degrees so his ass is in the girl's face and his legs are splayed across her shoulders and his back muscles are facing the crowd; his tongue's out, probing the floor for the rose. Someone from behind Ana cheers. He finds the rose. Everyone cheers. With the rose now between his teeth, he opens his eyes and starts surveying the crowd, winking and placing his hands on the ground, using them to rotate the chair, left to right then right to left, scanning—evading his gaze, Ana looks offstage, where it's only in broad strokes that she can see what's happening, so she misses the girl bring her head down, misses her settle her eyes on Ana and Mari, misses the recognition that flits across her face, but sees the tremendous ass slap she delivers to the boy, sees the boy pulling himself across the floor, sees him slithering toward them. She's looking now, there's no escaping it: he's coming. Does she know him? She doesn't. Does she know her?

Maya! The performers have stood up, walking side-by-side now, Maya on Ana's side, the man on Mari's, basically already there, Maya's reaching out her hand and feeling Ana's cheek. More cheers. Ana makes eye contact.

— Hi, — Ana whispers.

— Hello gorgeous.

The hand tightens and Ana blushes. She looks over at Mari, who's holding the rose in her mouth and tickling the man's chin. Cheers, cheers, cheers. Maya winks at Ana and then backs away, grabbing the man by the arm and leading him back to the chair.

The show's over. Ana and Mari are back in the hall, where the crowd seems to have thinned out a little. But it's really just the timing, Ana thinks, they're either late or early. She doesn't know which.

— The stars of the show!

Ana laughs,

— And what a handsome young man. Maybe I'll ask Maya to put y'all in touch.

— Ha! Maybe you and Maya should get in touch.

— If only. I think she's straight.

— She doesn't have to be!

— What?

Trying to sound like Ana,

— 'Everyone's a little gay, Mari,' — and seeing Ana's skeptical look, switching back, — is that not what you say?

— I mean . . . — Ana says, gesturing at Mari.

— No no no no no, that's not the same!

Ana laughs,

— Yeah, besides, I think I may have been wrong about that one.

Ana checks her phone. Nothing, some emails: a study at The Institute needs more participants, someone in her dorm is looking for AA batteries.

The crowd comes back into the hall.

— . . . and an essay and my reading and I have to write like fifteen cover letters . . .

— . . . I don't know, I've texted her like four times. Haven't heard anything but we need to cop . . .

— . . . all I'm saying is, if you want to do sexy performance art, then *do* sexy performance art but don't call it . . .

— . . . yeah saw it right before I came, like holy shit . . .

It's time. Ana and Mari enter the next room, where they're among the last in the crowd to arrange themselves around a trio of skinny, topless women facing away from the crowd, all wearing the same purple thigh-high heels and matching cowboy hats. They stand on a small, black stage.

The performers aren't moving; the crowd idles, chattering softly. Mari nudges Ana.

— You should get boots like that.

Ana considers her body.

— I don't think I-

But it's quiet now. One of the girls on stage has put her hand in the air.

A bassline is building.

They tap their boots.

Thirty seconds pass.

The girl lowers her hand, and the trio turns to face the crowd.

— We. Are. Girl Gang, — says one.

— So welcome to our show, — says another.

— And get ready to die! — says the third, beaming as the beat drops and all three girls, radiating confidence, scoop up their boobs and begin to fire into the crowd.

Well. Gunshots raining down from the speakers, the crowd cheering, the Girl Gang screaming at the crowd to fall over, the crowd falling over, sure enough, here it comes: the subject of tonight's test, what Ana had been secretly hoping she was past: dysphoria: looking at what she feels she can never be standing alongside what she knows she's never been, and now there's more cheering, more gunshots, more fucking feelings, thinks Ana, as she stands there, frozen, looking right into the eyes of Girl Gang member number 1, who's looking at her now and seeing that she's trans and calling out to her to come on up there and join the Girl Gang, and the crowd's cheering even louder now and Mari's cheering and she does the wrong thing, she does the wrong fucking thing, she thinks to herself as she sits in the bathroom stall, tears pooling in the palms of her hand, thinking that if she was going to make a scene, then she should've kicked off her giant shoes and stripped off her giant hoodie and gone up there with her receding hairline and her giant forehead and her giant shoulders, her cone tits, her nipple hair, her fat, her fucked up skin and her scars, and just screamed—but instead, she had stood there and cried, cried where everyone could see her and everyone could see that the Girl Gang girl was hurt and everyone could see Mari grabbing her by the shoulder and her running out of the room, everyone had seen her fail, Ana thinks; tonight, for all these cis people, she's representation: the sad tranny sitting in the bathroom stall, her friend Mari waiting anxiously in the hall, the drag show still going on, tears still pooling in the palms of her hand, Ana Turrón, feeling pathetic.

What she wants right now is a Demon, something she could grab by the throat and strangle. But looking around this University bathroom stall, Ana finds no Demon, only a stain, age-old and stall-wide, a mystery to even those most pensive of stall-goers, who have struggled, as Ana does now, looking for a way out of her head, to unravel its twin origin: somehow the sediment of generations of shit, piss, puke, cum, and blood, and yet, with equal plausibility, something that had surfaced from within the walls themselves, like the marks on the skin of a fruit filled with rotting flesh—well either way, it's there, and it's covered in scrawl, courtesy of those most expressive of stall-goers, who have given Ana something else to pour herself into, feeling now, more vividly than ever before, the impish glee and anonymous pain that's been registered on these walls using whatever was on hand: pencil; pen; loopy felt-tip; the violent scratch of a short, blunt key.

But just build a new fucking bathroom, Ana thinks.

— Ana?

Mari?

— Ana the show is almost over. We should-

— Yeah . . . I'm coming.

Ana stands up, wiping the last tears out of her eyes. She opens the stall door to a concerned-looking Mari.

— Ay, Ana . . .

Mari comes to give her a hug.

— Let's get out of here. — Ana says.

The two of them leave the bathroom and fly down the stairs, blowing past a few confused-looking co-op residents and exiting into the night.

It's brisk, outside. Brisk but nice.

As they walk down the patio steps, Ana checks her phone: one missed call from John Mung, fifteen minutes ago.

She laughs and shows Mari.

— But how desperate!

— I know, — says Ana, still laughing.

Mari's smoking again.

— Can I? — asks Ana.

— Should you? — asks Mari.

It's barely past ten. Ana and Mari are alone on the street, just a pair of red dots sitting at waist height, swaying home.

Carneval tomorrow. Rumor has it that a whole bunch of alumni are making their way back—a little birdie even said something about Johnny Soufflé making an appearance. Everyone's excited.

But it's Friday still. And Mari not knowing what to say, Ana not wanting to, our dynamic duo walk home in a silence broken only by the sound of an ambulance wailing into the night as it speeds past Ana and Mari, past the crowd now spilling out of the co-op, past that four-way stop at the center of campus nightlife, past the family of raccoons feasting in the fraternity dumpster, all the way out into the furthest reaches of campus, where somewhere behind the lake, a rattled jogger stands, pointing out into the darkness, waiting and watching nervously as the paramedics lift John Mung onto the stretcher and take him to the ambulance and back past the raccoons and the four-way stop and the now-dispersed crowd, there it goes, blaring right past the dorm of one Ana Turrón, who's curled up in bed, staring at her phone, doing her best not to think.

Saturday

We must prefer real hell to an imaginary paradise.
— SIMONE WEIL

Carneval

It's just one of those days, the kind where you wake up more or less completely in tune with the universe, vibrating at all the right frequencies—alive. Maybe you know. Maybe you've had one before. It's the kind of day where the self can't help but swell and soar; excess is the theme of the day, and it applies here, too: there's just too much self for one body to hold, so it decides to leave, roam out into the world, commune—vibe. Yes. It's a day worth living. A day of excess. The extra. That little something. Life. So maybe we can understand why this morning, of all mornings, our hero might wake up, touch the divine, and announce to the world,

— I'm Johnny Soufflé, and it's Carneval, baby.

The rumors are true. Johnny is back. But unbeknownst to the University rumor mill, Johnny is here on business: a single-day contract with The Student Liaison Office, who has asked Johnny to work Carneval, to liaison with the students and determine the 'pulse' of the student body. Johnny has been asked to do so discreetly, so as to observe an accurate 'pulse,' a decision no doubt informed by the wealth of research produced by the team of University researchers embedded in The Student Liaison Office, who, as Johnny has learned, in a few ad-hoc training sessions, have shown that there are in fact two student body 'pulses:' what those in the biz refer to as 'natch pulse,' the natural state of the student body, when unobserved; and 'liaise pulse,' the unnatural state of the student body, when demanding things from the administration.

Today's target is the natch pulse, which means Johnny is under strict orders not to reveal that he is attending Carneval in any sort of professional capacity—not that anyone would ask: it's not uncommon for recent grads, like Johnny, to attend Carneval, most having friends who were still undergrads, if they weren't themselves still University affiliated: finishing a fifth-year master's, starting a PhD, or spending their first year out of college otherwise adrift in University's orbit, working in one of the many administrative departments, living near campus, still seeing old friends, still semi-invested in the ongoings of their former world. Not our Johnny, though. He'd gone for a clean break. Today is the first time Johnny's been back to campus, and he's feeling good.

He's waiting in line at one of the campus coffee spots. It's early but the place is nevertheless popping: it's full of construction workers, who are being served breakfasts Johnny's never seen on the menu and bantering in friendly, teasing tones with the coffee shop employees, who, in mock exasperation, banter back—or so Johnny (monolingual) thinks; he's mostly going off the vibes. This is all basically new to him; he's never been here this early, having spent most of his undergraduate Saturday mornings laid up in recovery, paying off loans he had taken out the night before.

To say that Johnny is a man of debt would be both metaphorically and literally true: metaphorically, in the sense of the above, and literally, in the sense of owing some quarter of a million dollars to a combination of the federal government, several corporations, and University itself—Johnny being one of the first in a pilot program of University-backed student loans. And in fact, it's precisely this pilot program that explains why Johnny is here today: a little over a month ago, he had been approached by no less than The Office of the President, who had set him up with the single-day contract in exchange for some generous loan forgiveness—welcome news for Johnny, who had both an undying love for Carneval and, in his day, as a means of giving back, done his fair share of amateur liaising (successes include the designation of multiple public bathrooms as gender neutral, the installation of free pad and tampon dispensers in said bathrooms, and the lifting of the blanket ban on recreational bouncy castles).

Naturally enough, Johnny has wondered about this offer. It's true that none of the current Student Liaison Officers would be able to observe an accurate natch pulse, known as they are to the student body, but that doesn't particularly explain why they've picked Johnny, or why they're willing to forgive a year's worth of salary for a single day's work. Either the University administration is displaying an unprecedented level of interest in the mental well-being of its students, or somebody's scheming. Or maybe both. Johnny's not sure, and to be honest, doesn't really care. His report will be competent. He won't say anything the students don't want said, but he'll say enough to give the University administration something to think about. He'll see some old friends. He'll have a good time. Hello Carneval. Goodbye debt.

He orders a cappuccino and a pastry and retires to one of the coffee shop's couches, where he demolishes the pastry and waits patiently for his name to be called.

On the wall are a number of cartoon portraits depicting famous alumni: athletes, tycoons, movie stars, senators. Johnny has wondered about these people before, and presently, he wonders about them again: what were they like as students? were they stars then, too? Somehow, Johnny doubts it. It's entirely possible, maybe even likely, but still, Johnny doubts it: they clearly had other ambitions. And to be a University star, to be a campus legend, you had to want it and nothing else. This was the first lesson Johnny had been taught by his mentor, Alastair Torte; it was the first lesson Alastair Torte had been taught by his mentor, Carla Hamachi; it was the first lesson Carla Hamachi had been taught by her mentors, the Linguini twins; the Linguini twins had learned it from Arthur Scouse, Arthur Scouse from Moses Hog Jr., Moses Hog Jr. from Sofia Chuño, so on and so forth, the lin stretches back decades; it's tempting to call it a dynasty, but you're born into a dynasty, and if Alastair Torte and Carla Hamachi and the Linguini twins and Arthur Scouse and Moses Hog Jr. and Sofia Chuño and, indeed, Johnny Soufflé shared one quality, it was that they had earned their right to be campus royalty. You had to want it, you had to work for it, and you had to accept that at the end of the day, it meant nothing—those were Alastair's Three Maxims. Would a future senator dedicate four years of their life to nothing? Johnny doubts it.

You had to want it, you had to work for it, and you had to accept that at the end of the day, it meant nothing. Because at the end of the day, you graduate—and then? Sure, people still liked you; sure, you had connections; sure, there were upsides; but the life you'd built? Evaporated. Just like that. So you had to accept that it meant nothing. It was the only way you'd do anything, Johnny had said to his mentee, River Juice, early on in their tutelage: accept the fundamental meaninglessness of University social life, and it will open up before you as a space of radical possibility—you will do things you would have never dreamed possible. But do the opposite, cling to your success, and you will forever be its prisoner. It's like this, Johnny had explained, sagely, to the wide-eyed River, all of life boils down to two essential questions: are you having a ball? and are you feeling the love? River had not understood, and Johnny had not elaborated, a pedagogical trick he had learned from Alastair. River would come to understand Johnny's Two Questions, just as Johnny had come to understand Alastair's Three Maxims, and Alastair Carla's Principle of Reciprocated Truths, Carla the Linguini twins' Theory of the Metabolic Spliff, so on and so forth.

Today, Johnny thinks, as his name is called, and he collects his cappuccino, smiling at the barista, who smiles back, today, he is feeling the love. He is ready for the ball to begin.

□

But before the ball, business. Johnny has a check-in phone call with his contact at the Office of the President, who has specifically requested that Johnny make the call using what must be the only remaining payphone on campus, a relic of some bygone era, abandoned by time at the entrance of a West Campus parking lot, where Johnny now loiters, waiting to dial the number he's written down in his actual phone, staring out at one of the lawns in front of the West Campus dorms; a game of snappa is already underway. Though he is, of course, exceptionally skilled at them, the product of a prodigious natural talent and Alastair's brutal training regimen, Johnny does not like drinking games, having found that competition is anathema to both love-feeling and ball-having. No, Johnny prefers to drink intimately. It's a well-known fact that if Johnny Soufflé shows up at your door, wielding a sixer and his signature gap-tooth grin, then your night is about to get surreal, taking on that certain surreality that comes when you remember that your life is, in fact, real; that you only have one, and you're living it now. The abnormal tends to have this effect on people. You get used to the daily rhythms of your life. You stop hearing them. Then you hear something weird enough and remember you know how to listen. Such is a late-night conversation with Johnny Soufflé: weird enough.

One of the snappa players dives into the grass to catch a falling die. His teammate screams, appreciatively. Johnny checks his phone. He's still got a few minutes.

It's the sense that you're doing something. That's what Johnny likes about a good late-night conversation. He likes to make moves, a trait not typically associated with patience—indeed, enthusiasm—for long conversation, but this is one way in which Johnny believes we have done a great disservice to aspiring men—indeed, people—of action. Let's focus on men for now, though. Consider the great ones of history: Chicharrón, Jiaozi, Tonkotsu, Torte, and ask yourself whether any of them achieved any of the things they achieved without counsel, alone, closed off from the rest of the world. Did they exist as islands unto themselves? Were they only capable of dishing out laconic orders, issued as they brooded over what needed to be done? Here, again, Johnny is dubious. It seemed much more likely that history has simply forgotten that, transhistorically speaking, men everywhere depend on two groups for guidance: women, and the boys—two groups history has been more than happy to ignore. Which is to say, we have chosen to portray men of action as precisely this: islands unto themselves, only capable of dishing out laconic orders between broodings.

Johnny suspects that this is for the obvious reason that men are supposed to be neither vulnerable nor intimate—and there is nothing more vulnerable, or intimate, than a late-night conversation, particularly with Johnny Soufflé. If the eyes are the window to the soul, then the ears are surely the front door. So it's not just a disservice to men, women, and the boys, but a disservice to language itself, portrayed as somehow antithetical to move-making when, under the right circumstances, language becomes not only essential to action, but action itself: a force in the world.

Of course, Johnny thinks wistfully, checking his phone once again, and realizing he's a few minutes late, this conversation wasn't about to be like that—straight business. Strange there's no coin slot. He'd even brought quarters. Oh well. He punches in the numbers and waits.

— Hello? Johnny Soufflé here . . . feeling good, and how are you doing? . . . ebullient? — laughing, good-naturedly — you love to hear it . . . right . . . of course, down to business . . . yeah, the natch pulse . . . no that shouldn't be an issue . . . and when you say a 'diverse sample size' you mean . . . socially, got it . . . of course . . . no that shouldn't be an issue, I'm all about those representative demographics . . . uh huh . . . uh huh . . . well that was actually a question I had for you, seeing as it is the nature of the festivities . . . yeah . . . no doubt . . . I might even go as far as to say it's profligate, but I think to blend in appropriately, so as to observe the natch pulse, it'd be best to partake a little . . . yeah . . . of course . . . — laughing — no that shouldn't be an issue . . . right . . . and as for this report . . . uh huh . . . uh huh . . . naturally . . . right . . . of course . . . the thing is it'll be difficult to get all the way out here on short notice, what with the discretionary measures and all . . . you could always just text me . . . right . . . uh huh . . . well, sure . . . but . . . yeah . . . of course . . . you have my number . . . right . . . right . . . right on . . . right . . . hella . . . and if I need to contact you for whatever reason, is this number good? . . . okay, that was about everything I wanted to know, seems straightforward enough . . . yeah . . . sounds good . . . peace.

Johnny hangs up the phone. Things sounded a little hectic, over at The Office of the President—a little more hectic than usual, Johnny thinks, but that's probably to be expected, given the circumstances: Carneval, a day of profligate festivity, thousands of students out and about, drunk, high, excited, masked—anything could happen. And things would certainly be happening. Unless they've switched up the timing, The Lottery's only just finished, meaning that the student body is due for some much-needed catharsis.

And what a day to cathart, thinks Johnny, as he steps out onto the trail surrounding the lake. It's perfect, of course: sun supreme in the sky, temperature moderate, there's even a little bit of water in the lake, where little shards of sun dance as the water ripples in the wind—it's a shame he'd have to spend any of it inside. But inside is where he's headed, and not to celebrate either; he'd better wipe that grin off his face. Grinning and ebullient is no way to show up to a wake.

□

The bodies are laid out on a large mahogany table. The table belongs to Epsilon Chi Epsilon (or Ep-Chi), a fraternity found near the top of the Upper Row, close enough to the surrounding neighborhood to acquire a steady string of noise complaints and, in one memorable incident, a bit of professorial direct action involving a pair of garden shears, several thousand dollars worth of damage to audio equipment, no pressed charges, and, come finals, one exceedingly generous curve.

The table is nearly as old as Ep-Chi itself, having belonged to the initial class of '21, and having weathered just about everything since. Whatever sheen the table originally had has since washed away in several oceans worth of spilled beer, hammered into the table by the equivalent in clumsy dancing. To say that it's sticky would be testing the limits of understatement. It goes without saying that the table has never been cleaned, a point of pride for the Ep-Chi brethren, twelve of whom now lay across it, each wearing their worst suit and a hand-decorated tie whose designs Johnny would be sure to appreciate but can't, presently, make out on account of the light situation: a single dim lamp and some heavy-duty curtains, drawn over the windows.

— Boys, — begins the speaker, — gentlemen. We are gathered here today in eulogy for the twelve men you see before you, from left to right: Chet, Chaz, Chase, Alkirk, Ali, Enrique, Joey, Little Mike, Dirty Dave, Marshall, Vadim, and Second Chaz. No doubt each of you is here today because, in some way or another, these men have exerted a profound influence on the course of your life. To do justice to each of these fine specimens would require time we do not have, and oratory skills I do not possess, for even the most silver-tongued of devils could not spin yarn adequate to the memory of these here, the deceased. But we should say a few words. For this is it, boys. Death. The big kahuna. No doubt you're already familiar with the usual thanatopical discursions, and what else to add here? Surely, you already know that death comes for us all. Surely, you are already aware that in the vast expanse of ecological—nay, cosmological—time, our time here is but less than a blip, so insignificant as not to even register. Surely, it has not escaped you that one of the key features of death is that you stay dead, infinitely; that there is no coming back; that death is final in only the most exacting and relentless sense of the word. Surely you have thought of all this before and even now, as you're hearing the words come out of my mouth, you are dismissing them; whatever part of your brain registers these thoughts has long since hardened, covered in an impenetrable carapace of cope. I don't blame you. How else could you live? The short answer is: you couldn't. Memento mori on the mind is no way to live, and we do like to live, don't we, boys? No one more so than the twelve men laying before us. Four years of indefatigable life outta these fine gentlemen, no question about that. They lived to booze and boozed to die. Gentlemen! I can sense that my time is also coming to a close. So let me just call attention to the fact that before us, prostrate on this fine, marvelous table, are twelve testaments to nothing less than life itself. And as we prepare to send them from this world into the next, let us all pause and take a second to meditate on these twelve lives well lived . . . now, PLEDGES! — twelve boys line up in front of the table, each holding a thirty-rack in one hand, and a single can in the other, — if you please.

Each of the twelve boys drops the thirty-rack onto the floor, reaches into their pocket for a key, and holds their beer aloft.

— For duty.

The twelve boys shotgun their beers.

— For honor.

They shotgun a second.

— For sacrifice.

A third, sending a few of the freshmen to the floor.

— And with that, boys, let the Deinitiation begin.

With the exception of Dirty Dave, who seems to be stuck,

the Ep-Chi senior class manages to sit up and hop off the table, reaching into their provided thirty-rack and withdrawing their first beer—the remaining twenty-six to be drunk over the course of the day, per Deinitiation ritual.

— Is that Johnny motherfucking Soufflé?

Johnny turns and has just enough time to brace himself for a high-velocity hug.

— Mia! It's been too long.

Mia backs out of the hug,

— And whose fault is that?

— Dunno . . . Death's?

— Ugh, fucking Jedidiah. Well, you picked a good day for a resurrection. It's gonna be a wild one, sounds like.

— More than the usual?

— Oh yeah, big plans, — she says, impishly.

— Right on. But hey, what are you doing in a frat? I'm remembering a certain late-night resolution . . .

Flushing a little,

— Didn't think you'd remember that . . . yeah, I know, but I promised Ali I'd come.

— Me too, actually, and, — looking around, — well shit if he isn't-

— Johnny motherfucking Soufflé, — says Ali Barg, dapping Johnny up, — back from the dead at long last. How *are* you, bro?

— Feeling a little effervescent this morning . . . and who's this? — gesturing at the haggard-looking freshman trailing Ali, carrying one of the thirty-racks.

— Johnny motherfucking Soufflé, meet Ricky Beerboy.

— Is that hyphenated?

— Ricky, beer me.

Ricky hands Ali a fresh beer.

— Ah.

— Well you're lucky, Ricky, — says Mia, — Ali here's a real softie.

Ricky looks doubtful, but no one is looking at Ricky.

—So what's good? How's it being back?

— It's wild, feels like-

— ALI! — hollers Second Chaz from across the room, — The Inner Sanctum requests your presence.

— Shit. I should go. Listen, I'll catch you later, alright?

— No worries.

— COMING BROTHER! — Ali hollers back, as he strides across the room, Ricky in tow.

— Don't know how Ali does it. All these white boys.

— Seems like he's thriving.

— The drinking. The hazing. The stench, — wrinkling her nose, — god it smells like death in here.

— It being a wake and all.

Mia rolls her eyes.

— Should we bounce then? — says Johnny.

— Let's bounce! I was going to drop by Iremia, if you want to tag along?

— Sure . . . and what sort of plans do you have for that?

— This? — asks Mia, plucking the joint out from behind her ear, — J on the way?

Johnny smiles, enthusiastically, and the two head to the door and out into the street, where they pass the joint back and forth as Mia catches Johnny up on the most recent developments in her life: her apprenticeship under the field's leading eco-statistician, the job she got, the coworkers she's already met, the friends she'll miss, the romances she won't. They manage to cover a lot of ground by the time they've made it down the Row and onto the Iremia lawn, where Mia pauses to say hi to one of her friends, and the now rather pleasantly stoned Johnny can't help but listen in to the conversation drifting down from one of the balconies,

— I just think that like as a society, we could just acknowledge that smoking cigarettes is cool. That we can like take coolness and reduce it to a set of behaviors, and practices, and rituals, and chief among those behaviors and practices and rituals is smoking cigarettes. Like it's just a fact that smoking cigarettes makes you cooler. It's a key feature of being cool.

— Isn't the idea that it doesn't have to be?

— But it does! That's what I'm saying. Coolness exists. It's like, a real thing. A real thing with history and like describable components. I don't think we can just change it to be whatever we want.

— Isn't the idea that we can?

— I really don't think so! They've been trying. But it can't be done. The cigarette just is cool.

— I dunno. For example, if we were to smoke a cigarette now to try to be cool, wouldn't that make us uncool?

— Maybe, but that's only because we're trying, which is obviously as antithetical to coolness as smoking cigarettes is like thetical.

— I'm still not sure. For example, if we were to smoke

cigarettes and constantly talk about the act of smoking cigarettes, wouldn't that also make us uncool?

— Maybe, but okay all I'm saying is if we want to make it 'cool' not to smoke, it'd probably be easier to make a whole new affect than to try to tell people smoking isn't cool.

— Is it an affect? or is it an abstract and mutable relationship to social capital? For example-

— Earth to Johnny.

Johnny blinks.

— Stoned out of his mind already. You're such a lightweight!

— I was just-

— Doesn't matter. Let's head inside, yeah? I've got a surprise for you.

□

Whatever the surprise is, it's through the kitchen, which is looking like a formidable obstacle at the moment, at least to Johnny, who really has no desire to get in the way of what's happening before him, preparations, he's sure, for The Grand Feast, that great Carneval tradition wherein all of the co-ops, and a few of their friends, hike up the hill and gather in the Palma backyard, each bringing their own mountain of home-made food, plus drink, plus whatever else looks fun—bit of a free-for-all, The Grand Feast, though not without its organizational charms: Johnny's never seen The Spreadsheet, but he's heard tell; no doubt there's a series of color-coded columns governing the very chaos stretching out before him, which Mia seems to be navigating with expert ease, dancing through the line of vegetable choppers, between the nervous-looking boys carrying stock pots full of broth, past the couple expertly scoring a whole host of batards, and onto the door, where her near-perfect execution is stopped by two residents carrying what looks to be a pair of rather large legs, though Johnny (pescatarian, near-sighted) can't be sure.

— Well? — Mia yells from across the kitchen, and now it's Johnny's turn to tango, though he's boldly choosing to go on the left side of the massive island at the center of the kitchen, taking him past some sautérs, one ambitious flambé, and now the pair of residents carrying what Johnny confirms are legs as he shimmies by them and around the open door of one of the industrial-size refrigerators, where a curly-haired goddess stands, staring in evident frustration at what looks to be a cardboard box half full of butter—or maybe a butter substitute, thinks Johnny, as he finally greets Mia on the other side, and the two exit the kitchen and head up a few flights of stairs to Mia's room.

— Johnny	— Johnny	— Johnny
motherfucking	motherfucking	motherfucking
Soufflé!	Soufflé!	Soufflé!

— Fellas, how are we today?

| — Good. | — Good. | — Dogshit. |

— Don't listen to him.

— He's in a mood.

— You would be too.

— What happened? — asks Johnny, looking for a seat.

| — Dumped. | — Dumped. | — Nothing. |

— Sorry to hear that.

— They didn't dump me. They just said they wanted to talk.

— But the dumping is imminent.

— They've never wanted to talk before.

— In fact, I didn't even know they could talk.

— They've said maybe six words in our presence.

— If that.

— 'This. Is. Dead. Should. I. Roll. Another,' — says Mia, counting out the words on her fingers, — that's seven, I think.

— They're just shy.

— They're stuck up.

— They're not stuck up, you just have to get to know them.

— If they weren't stuck up, we would know them. But they are, — sighing, theatrically, — yet another skinny, white, rich-

— I'm skinny, white, rich. You're skinny, white, rich.

— Yeah but not in the same way.

Here Johnny (fat, mixed-race, middle-class) misses a look of desperate solidarity from Mia, riveted as he is by the current discussion. Everyone knows Johnny is an insatiable gossip: never malicious, always invested, more of a consumer than a disher, though he's been known to dish when dishing is called for. It's probably fair to say that in his four years at University, Johnny was the gossip king of campus; his penchant for late-night conversation, selectively encyclopedic memory, and ever-expanding network of friends meant that Johnny was, benevolently, up in just about everyone's shit—although he was more of a historian than a meddler, so perhaps less up in and more up on?

— I'm just saying maybe if they talked to us, we wouldn't think they were stuck up. Like if they talked half as much as their roommate-

— A tenth as much as their roommate.

— A tenth as much as their roommate, then we'd be fine with them.

— It's not that they don't seem nice.

— They do seem nice.

— Just kind of a stuck up bitch.

— A little bit of a stuck up bitch!

— And we're happy for you, Xay.

— Obviously we're happy for you.

— But we are your friends.

— And it's our duty-

— Our imperative.

— To be honest with you when you need it.

— So Johnny, — says Mia, wisely choosing to interrupt, — what do you know about Tr-Y?

— I've heard it's a bit like acid, only . . . more? Tried it once but the batch we had was busted. Didn't do anything.

— Well, — Mia says, lifting a mint tin off her desk, opening it, and removing a piece of a blotter, — surprise! This batch works. I get it straight from this Chem PhD who synthesizes it herself.

The tin travels around the circle and arrives at Johnny. One tab left. Decision time. He has a job to do, and he hasn't forgotten it. Not that he's particularly concerned about the job itself; while it's true the job he's been asked to do appears to require a level of clear-eyed perception, one, Johnny is already fairly high, and two, Johnny belongs to that species of human who believe that certain flavors of drug work not by distorting our perception but by righting it, believing that in fact it is our everyday perception that is distorted and irregular, and that one way, among a few, of countering these irregular distortions, and bringing us closer to reality, is the use of a powerful psychedelic—if University wanted Johnny to produce penetrating insights into the state of the student body, well, it'd certainly get them. No, what Johnny's concerned about is his trip: nothing ruins a good time like the lingering sense of obligation, which is why Johnny has organized every single one of his trips around periods of freedom, whether that be vacations, or, in one period of his life, mid-to-late sophomore year, Saturdays, when Johnny, through efforts hellacious and organizational schemes abstruse, had managed to order his life such that his Saturdays were really, truly free: not a trace of homework, or work, or chores, or social appointments, or anything else that could interfere with the kinds of psychonautical exploration of which Johnny is so fond.

But now that he's spent a little too long staring at the tin, something else is occurring to Johnny: isn't his task today precisely the sort of extrospective adventure that a healthy dose of Drugs might engender? Here he's been conceptualizing the two—trip and task—as fundamentally antagonistic, but it might be the case that there's actually some synergy here. Observe, ruminate, and report. That was his task, and hadn't the people from the Student Liaison Office said something about ORR requiring that you situate yourself in a certain kind of radical authenticity? What could be more authentically Carneval . . . ?

Fuck it, then. He's in. He puts the last piece of the blotter on his tongue.

— That's the Johnny I know.

He passes the mint tin back to Mia and pulls out his phone to begin the timer.

00:00:00

The discussion continues. Xay needs to text his partner back, but what to say? Yes, he's free to talk, but can it wait until tomorrow, he's just taken some Drugs, or, maybe, he'd already started tripping when he saw this—better, better—and he doesn't want that to cheapen their talk. Good. He sends the text and an almost immediate response of 'sure.' sends the room into maximum overdrive: 'sure.'? '.'?? Oh they're mad, they have to be mad, ugh, maybe he should go talk with them now, but the Tr-Y would kick in in thirty minutes, and West Bog is a fifteen minute walk, seven and a half if they split the distance, but R. has a thing about having talks where other people could hear them, so it'd have to be one of their rooms—not here, babe—ugh.

Xay stews for a few more minutes and then, with a little help from his friends, relaxes. Johnny smiles. He's missed this. Not that his life in the city is particularly bereft of happenings, but it all lacks a certain narrative cohesion: the gossip is too diffuse, too sparse; here, the drama's dense: the main arcs;

the backstories; the side characters, who weave in and out, their own arcs unfurling into sagas of their own; the stakes; the rising; the falling; that centrifugal yank that sends one out of one friend group and hurling into the next, or maybe just into a single new friend, the two spinning round and round and round, their revolutions accelerating, unstable; maybe it's a pair of disappointed lovers ejecting out of a collapsing relationship and rocketing about as they mourn, heal, and learn to love again; or maybe they're infusing the relationship with new life: a third, a fourth, a fifth, a sixth? well here's a romantic geometry he's never seen before, something new for the archive; Johnny's never been morally opposed to relationship anarchy, but he does have a few formal objections: these things have hidden structures, their own laws of motion, constants, variables, all to be discovered through that messiest of sciences: love . . .

— You said this stuff takes thirty minutes to hit?

Mia looks at Johnny, bemused.

— Give or take. How are you feeling?

— Groovy, — says Johnny, smiling and tilting his head back, — real groovy.

The room laughs. They're all feeling a little giddy. Something in their stomachs. The Drugs, probably, though it's not outside the realm of possibility that some of what Johnny is feeling right now is that cappuccino, making itself known. It has, he reflects, been extraordinarily patient; he knows better than to test its generosity.

He gets up, mentions something about a bathroom, and heads there. It's empty, much to Johnny's relief. He's looking forward to some repose.

And he finds it, at least for a minute or two before something starts to tickle him out of his thoughts: he's not alone. Ants, hundreds, march down from a hole in the ceiling, down the wall, over the graffiti, under the sheets of poetry, and onto the floor, where they seem to be collecting . . . was that . . . hair? Johnny leans in. Not just hair, skin too, and little flecks of shit—not his, he doesn't think—eyelashes, fingernails, scabs, a blood-soaked booger, nose hair curling out—it even seems, to Johnny's eyes, that these ants were somehow reliquifying what had long since become floor: how else to explain the globule of piss mounted on this ant's back, surface tension threatening to give way as it struggles up the wall and back into the hole in the corner, back to the colony, where these ants must be assembling something, all this human detritus, all this residue, studied, understood, weaponized, turned on the residuer, nature's revenge, a debt owed, a debt paid—was there time to rally the troops? could he speak to them, somehow, through the pipes, the others, the toilet-bound, just how many of them were there? right now, plugged into the porcelain, ready to heed his call, members of some unacknowledged communion, allies in the war to come . . . and it's come: Johnny's been conscripted, all our children have, off to fight The Enemy Within; deep in the offices of the war machine, difficult decisions have been made: there simply wasn't enough money; taxes had to increase; services had to be gutted; the other wars, all seven, had to end; the troops were flown home, and with no one left to staff them, approximately eight hundred overseas bases were closed down; what a shame, the world had said, but there was no time to reassure them of imminent return, the ants had already invaded the countryside, where Johnny's been sent: someone has to take care of the bodies, burn them, make sure there's nothing left for the ants to recover . . . but he's too late: eye sockets, emptied and teeming with ants stare back at him, shimmering in the heat.

The door to the bathroom opens, and Johnny is wrenched back into the present. Here we go. He's tripping, alright. Something about bathrooms always sets Johnny off. He doesn't know what, but it's preferable to the alternative, he thinks, as he does his best not to listen to the retching two stalls over. The door to the bathroom opens again.

— Priya? Why'd you run in . . . oh, honey.

The retching stops and is replaced with a soft murmur Johnny can't understand. He exits the stall and goes to the sink, where he uses the mirror to assess the situation.

Priya's sitting up now, at least, though that murmur's blown well past babble somewhere into the vicinity of flood, leaving Johnny with precious seconds to grab hold of something concrete in the swirl of her thoughts—cigarettes, coolness, the obvious health concerns—before he's completely swept up. And thank god he did. Priya's spewing something fierce, and not just a bit jargonic. She's already begun to gesture towards a question, a provocation, and there's no telling what will happen when she starts staging encounters with much-needed interventions—Johnny's just barely managing to keep his head above water as is. And it is just barely: binaries are being troubled, aporias dodged; this bathroom is full of wanton problematization. So it's no surprise that when a few floating futurities come his way, Johnny's relieved, something to cling to as he bobs rhythmically in the waves of her thought, his eyes trained on the horizon, where he sees her diagramming something on the bathroom wall—the clear sign of a thinker in distress. Johnny'd better do something.

— She okay? — he asks.

— Does she seem okay? — says the friend. — Too much Tr-Y. It's her first time.

— Yeah, mine too.

— Hmm. You seem . . . fine.

— Uh huh, — says Johnny, who's just spied another platoon of ants making its way down the wall. — Did she get the Tr-Y from Mia?

— I dunno.

— She'll know what to do. I'll get her.

Johnny gets Mia, who assesses the situation.

— Yeah, she's had too much.

— What do we do?

— Two options: we wait, and let her burn out; or we give her some Pr-X, which should ease the trip.

— You've got some?

— Yeah.

— Well get it!

Mia gets the Pr-X, which, after some difficulty, she manages to convince Priya to take.

They wait a few minutes while Priya eases.

— Priya? You good?

Priya rubs her eyes.

— Think so.

Her friend sighs, relieved.

— How much did you take?

— Just a tab.

— Normal dose?

— Think so. He said to take one.

— Who's he?

— The guy that sold it to us. Jake or Jeff or Josh or something. I don't know. He doesn't go here. Works in the area. Farah knows him. Sold us a bunch. Sorry, — says Priya, suddenly aware of her company, — aren't you Johnny motherfu-

— The one the only, — says Mia, — Priya baby I'm going to need to borrow some of your Tr-Y.

— What? Why?

— You shouldn't have been tripping that hard off a single tab, even if it was your first time. We should get it tested.

— Really?

— Yeah.

— Fine. There's some in my room.

— Shall we? — says Johnny, who's just about had enough of this bathroom.

They head to Priya's room and collect a tab; Mia and Johnny exit into the hall.

— I'm going to take this to my friend. Come with?

Johnny starts to say something about a diverse sample size.

— This'll be quick, I promise.

Well why not, thinks Johnny, looking at his phone, it's only noon.

— Do you have your mask?

— Right here, — he says, removing his Carneval mask from an orange drawstring bag.

— We're good then.

Johnny checks the timer.

00:37:53

The duo stride out the Iremia doors—well, Mia's striding, Johnny here's somewhat lackadaisical; he prefers a stroll, especially when his mind is busy, as it currently is, wrestling with the passage of time. Just never seems to stop being interesting: first it's slow, then it's fast, then it's slow again, a fascinating subject, one Johnny will have plenty of time to study, later, when there's less to look at: Carneval's in full swing, and Johnny's seeing in panorama: out past a lawn thick with hecklers, the masses swirl in the street, looking for a darty— ah but which one? Johnny begins to disaggregate the mass by clothes. Here the beach-bound, elsewhere, the foam-ready, yet further, the pagans. What other avatars would the darty find itself in today? Who has summoned it? And what did they want? Across the street, Johnny spots a petting zoo; to its left, he can't help but feel a little proud to see, a bouncy castle, smoke oozing out its mesh sides; between them, more costumes: evidently one of the houses is feeling a little religious, or sacrilegious, Johnny supposes, as Mia leads him past a priest, a rabbi, and an imam, who seem to be in the middle of some sort of punch line, at whose front is a rather tall nudist, carefully ladling liquid death into a red cup. Velour tracksuits; fits nautical and galactic, urban and pastoral; there are references to movies he's seen, books he's skimmed, and shows he's halfway through, but where Johnny's eye is drawn, today, is the unaffiliated, the nondescript. It's Johnny's experience that nondescription is the mark of Carneval neophytes and Carneval aficionados alike—a common enough pattern, two sides of a bell curve, both doing the same thing in totally different ways, one ignorant, almost accidental, the other knowledgeable, intentional. Here the intention is mobility. You want to be able to move between the parties with ease—or, at any rate, that's Johnny's contention. There are different philosophies, of course. Johnny cut his teeth in Alastair's school, an idiosyncratic blend of party miniaturism, value-dorm theory, and second-wave feminism—Carneval in One Party, a noble enough pursuit, but not exactly to Johnny's tastes. For Alastair, it was about party perfection, a singular expression of the Carneval spirit, but for Johnny ... for Johnny, there is no singular expression; the Carneval spirit can only be expressed in multiplicity, in diversity. Isn't that, in the end, what this whole thing's about? Less a spirit and more a potential, kaleidoscoped into a thousand different blooms, each unique, each free. Johnny just wants to see everyone thriving. And what better occasion? It's a time for celebrating: the Lottery is over; a new world's on the way. And like any new world, this one's not arriving from without—dropped off at their doorstep, neatly wrapped and ready to go—but rather, from within: University's about to molt. Finals loom. Summer follows. Whatever surprises are left in store for the year, they'll have to happen soon. The year's almost fully calcified, less dynamic flesh, more hard husk, ready to be cast off by the great University beast as a new year emerges, fresh and full of promise. But it's not calcified yet. There's still time for one last ball. And *that*, Johnny thinks, is what it's all about: having a ball, feeling the love. Because Jedidiah is right. We all die. We all fucking die, and then we spend the rest of eternity dead. And that means one of two things needs to happen: either we figure out how not to die, or we figure out how to live. Leave immortality to the scientists, Johnny here's something of a humanist, which means he's mostly concerned with option two, emphasis on the *we*. Because life is a collective affair, isn't it, and that means that learning to live can't be a process of individual adjustment; it can't be a new mentality; it can't be diet and exercise; it can't be a mantra; it is, and can only be, a revolution, the total restructuring of society as we know it, taking a however-millennia-long cult of death and obliterating it, sandblasting every last stain off the face of this earth. Whew. Johnny's not normally an especially political guy. It just seems to him now that basically all of human history can be summarized as follows: things were alright, and then they were bad, and they're still bad, so let's make them good, quickly, before we destroy the entire fucking planet. Sure, Johnny's getting a little liberal with his *we*'s here, but the fact of the matter is that while we may not all be responsible for the ongoing destruction of the earth, we are responsible for preventing it. Because the people who are responsible won't. Not can't. Won't. And why would they? They're already having a ball. But they are not feeling the love. And this is exactly why there are *Two* Questions! Whole empires have been built on loveless ball-having—hell, look no further: here we are, after all, at University, the empire's crown jewel, doing Drugs and having a ball while, off in foreign lands, our government rains death on unsuspecting civilians, and starves the rest, their sanctions paving the way for multinational vampires to swoop in and drain the land, the nature, the people, whatever they can find, really, bloodlust being a hopelessly weak metaphor for the viciousness of this flavor of greed, which we don't even need to study abroad to see, since we've got it right here at home, even here, on the University campus, where we now sit, right at the tippy top of the meat grinder, doing Drugs and having a ball. No doubt, thinks Johnny, but this isn't his first rodeo: a well-kept secret, known only to a select few late-night conversationalists, is that Johnny's sophomore year Carneval was quite a bad trip indeed, and that he had spent the remaining weeks disillusioned and disgusted, with himself, with Carneval, with University. It was Alastair who had saved him from himself, one final piece of wisdom before he graduated: it's what you feel. Johnny sat on these four words all summer. It's what you feel. It's what you feel. And what was it Johnny felt? Disgusted? Disillusioned? Angry? Guilty? Ashamed? Grateful. Grateful for the life he had, a life he had fought for, a life he had—once, years ago—decided not to end. It was then, sitting on that green couch, as sober as you can be, that Johnny first felt the love. The love is a love unlike any other. Other loves deal in discrimination. They select a person, a thing, a people, a place, and they separate it, make it special. But not the love. The love suffuses everything. It is thoroughly cosmic, existential, concerned not with any one being but with being itself, with life. Understand that the love is dangerous. It can break you. Because when you feel the love, when you apprehend the phrase 'the gift of life' in all its infinite profundity, when you return from your transcendence and emerge into the real world, you will immediately see how much of your everyday existence is death. You will see that there is a war being fought on life, and that life is losing. And you will feel completely and utterly helpless. But then you will remember that every war has two sides. You will remember the times you felt alive. Carneval, for Johnny, is one such time: an expression of life. So that's what Johnny is seeing today: a life that was once his own, and that had now gone on without him. Yes, long after his graduation, when the name Johnny Soufflé meant nothing, when his friends' names meant nothing, when everyone he knew had passed on into a new life, and everything that had seemed so important, that still seems so important, had faded into nothingness, it would still be here: University, Carneval, life. There would still be friends, there would still be gossip, there would still be late nights spent conversating, teetering on the precipice of some great change, it would all still be there. Sure, when the day comes, University will change; it'll be abolished, replaced with something new, better, fairer, more free, but it'll still be there, and somehow, someway, Johnny will be a part of it. They all will.

— Are you . . . crying?

— Yes, — Johnny says, as he and Mia pass under the archway and leave Carneval behind, — yes I am.

Mia smiles. Drugs. She's seen weirder, especially from Johnny. They walk in pleasant silence.

— Are you feeling anything yet? — he asks.

— A little bit. How long's it been?

— Let me check.

00:39:31

— Damn, Tr-Y doesn't fuck around.

— Yeah, you can thank Rachele, — Mia says, opening the door to The Institute. Johnny looks around. Everything has a sort of blood-drenched tint to it.

— Atrocious vibes in here.

—You're seeing it too, huh?

— Yeah.

— Drugs?

— Drugs.

The two burst into laughter and zoom through The Institute lobby. It's a minefield in there, especially for the Tr-Y-addled, but Mia's a pro and Johnny's a fast learner; they manage to make it to the lab unscathed.

— Rachele, Johnny motherfucking Soufflé; Johnny motherfucking Soufflé, Rachele.

— Hey.

— Howdy.

— So, you had some Tr-Y you wanted me to look at?

— Yeah, here, — handing Rachele the tab, who grabs it, carefully, with a pair of forceps and moves to a nearby station, where she drops the tab in a beaker of clear liquid, which, soon enough, turns a berserk yellow.

— Thought so.

— What's that mean?

— It's cut with Hege-M.

— Hege-M?

— Fascinating compound. Basically it neutralizes the c-fetishnylase in Tr-Y by binding to your MECW receptors, which stops histmatine reuptake, and that's no good because basically . . . so inside your neurons you have this thing called a DotB complex, which sends the Hege-M along what's called the MCM' pathway to a couple different ISA reticula, and the ISA reticula are where your brain makes certain amino acid chains, but if Hege-M is in the picture, then you've got a whole bunch of M chains and ML chains and MLM chains and MLMpM chains with nowhere to go, so they start degenerating, which is bad because . . . well so really what happens depends on whether or not you have any MoP, which most people don't, but some people do, and it's a neurotransmitter that triggers a LARP flood when you take Tr-Y, which you don't want, because of this whole thing with AES cofactors and the way they interact with FALC sites, which can turn into this whole thing since the thing about Tr-Y is that-

— Rachele, is it dangerous?

— What, Hege-M? No, totally harmless. Kind of the whole point. Some people think it's safer. I mean it has some side effects, like schizophasia, that's the word salad you saw, but that's only because there's this whole thing with-

— Hate to interrupt but could I bum a cigarette off either of y'all? Feeling a little jittery.

— Sure, — says Rachele, offering one up.

— Obliged, — says Johnny, grabbing it. — Mia, I'll meet you outside . . . which would be what way again?

— Go out the door, take a left, a right, go up the stairs,

take another right, a third right, and then the stairs again.

— Right on, — says Johnny, opening the door, taking a left, a right, going up the stairs, taking another left, another right, and opening the door, which, by the time Johnny's realized his mistake, has already locked behind him.

He's still outside, at least, somewhere near the back of The Institute. A ramp leads to the road above, where an unmarked van idles—no sign of the driver.

Johnny walks up the ramp and looks for somewhere to loiter. University law stipulates that all smoking happen thirty feet from any building, but Johnny's just looking for a good bench (though relatively well-versed in University lore, Johnny is blissfully unaware of the bureaucratic bloodbath necessary to pass such a law, which—for something that is so rarely observed, and perhaps even more rarely enforced—resulted in so much honest-to-god trauma that even the most indignant of smokers might think twice about ignoring it, if for no other reason than to pay their respects to the real human anguish that took place in those two some years; the dustbin of history is littered with the laments of the forgotten, indeed).

Bench found, Johnny now sits, holding the cigarette, pensively. It's a shame they kill you. He'd had a professor once who had pointed out that the cigarette was one of, if not the only, product that when used as designed, killed you. That must be part of the appeal, thinks Johnny, who's only scantly familiar with the notion of a death drive, and thus a little hesitant to deploy it here, but who suspects, nevertheless, that something is up with his good friends life and death, both of whom seem to be deeply invested in the object he now holds:

death, for billions of obvious reasons; and life, for . . . fewer, less obvious reasons, but reasons nonetheless: how much of what Johnny generally considers living happens near and around the cigarette?

He rolls the end of the cigarette between his fingers, loosening a bit of the packed tobacco, which drops out the end of the cigarette, onto the ground. He's thinking.

He's thinking that more cynical minds than he might see a rhapsodical enthusiasm for smoking as something like a bourgeois affectation; this on the empirical grounds that most people who smoke don't actually like it. That would mean the smokers Johnny met in his four years at University are not a particularly representative bunch, but this should come as no surprise, thinks Johnny, as he looks up and out at the campus: University is not a particularly representative school. Most college students don't live on campuses like this one; most college students don't live on campuses at all; most students commute; most students work; many do not have enough food; many are unwell; they are precarious, and feeling it, an experience not entirely foreign to some members of the University student body, thinks Johnny, as he begins to feel that familiar drop in his stomach, like he's mid-nosedive, being dragged by the gravity of his thoughts into some tripper's abyss, where he's sure to have a bad time. He breathes. Does he want to have a bad time? Not really. Not today. Not on Carneval. It's not for nothing that he's trained himself to recognize this feeling. He has to take control, retrace his thoughts: precarity . . . crumpled illusions . . . bourgeois affectations . . . cigarettes. Right. Cigarettes.

He looks again at the cigarette in his hand. Johnny himself's what you might call a casual smoker, meaning that he really only smokes when otherwise fucked up and doesn't spend all too much time thinking about it. But of course, he's also a hobnobber, and, having spent many a hobnob hobnobbing with some of the country's most enthusiastic smokers, bourgeois and not, it shouldn't be all too surprising that today, Johnny's not exactly wanting for riffing material. Take, for instance, the sermon he'd once heard from a dear friend about how the cigarette is the closest thing modern society has in the way of a short-term cure for mental illness; he's forgotten most of the details, but the gist seems workable, if a little fraught: does Johnny really want to be thinking about mental illness right now? Better nip that one in the bud. What else, what else? There was Priya's conversation from earlier, but how much more was there really to think about that? Priya's right, of course. Smoking is cool, granted you don't wax or otherwise think too hard. It's glamorous. It's sexy. It kills you, in a cool, glamorously sexy way. Hmm. Death again. Always death. But wouldn't it be nice if—hold on—yes— yes!—YES!—ok, here it comes: Johnny can feel it: the idea, roaring into existence: the cancer-free cigarette.

Imagine: President Soufflé, surfing into office on a tremendous wave of left-populism. Just one campaign promise: the invention, nationalization, and mass distribution of the cancer-free cigarette. He wins in a landslide. First day of his presidency he wastes no time. Doesn't even bother swearing in. Too busy. Has to secure funding. Signs a ceasefire with the ants. That's good. No more military. Excellent. No more police, either. Even better. Hard to have prisons with no police. Good riddance. Big tobacco? Nationalized. Private healthcare? Too expensive. Nationalized. Alright. Now we're cooking. Plenty of cash to go around, even after reparations. So call up science. Tell em we've got work to do. Some people are skeptical. That's fine. Set up a propaganda ministry. Put those humanities degrees to work. Full employment. Not bad. Fuck it! Twenty-hour work week. Good time to go green. It's train season, baby. Ring, ring, ring. Science on the phone. They've just discovered the cancer-free cigarette. Arts flourish. Worker solidarity's taking off. They start organizing. Good. Let em. Let's get this withering away started. Presidency thing's kind of a drag. So fast forward. State's gone. Class too. Abolished a bunch actually. All in the people's hands now. Hell yeah. Take it away, people.

It'd be that easy, thinks Johnny. Political slam dunk. It's too bad all the politicians are—

His phone buzzes.

It's too bad all the politicians are—

It buzzes again.

— Mia? . . . yeah, I'm in the back . . . yeah, by the old arts library . . . there's a bench, you'll see me . . . for sure . . . ok . . . see you soon.

Should probably smoke this thing, thinks Johnny, searching his pockets. Ahh. No lighter. Comical. Mia'll have one.

A minute passes, serenely. Johnny looks at his phone.

01:50:01

What?

01:50:03

That can't be right.

01:50:06

— Johnny!

— Mia man how long have we-

— Yeah, — Mia says, — a while. It really started hitting when I was in the lab.

— Yeah?

— Just thinking about the earth. How they're killing her. Have you been sitting here this whole time?

— I solved politics.

— Add it to the list.

(Here Mia is referring to our intrepid polymath's knack for solving big problems, things like, e.g., gender, which, it turns out, is pretty simple: you're either using gender or gender is using you, as Johnny is wont to say, so don't be a mark.)

— You feeling good? — Mia asks.

— Yeah.

— Lucid?

— Sure.

— Good. We're gonna be busy.

— Yeah?

— I just don't get it. Why go to the trouble of cutting all this Tr-Y?

— Didn't Rachele say it was safer?

— You saw what happened to Priya.

— True. Maybe it's cheaper, let's them sell more.

— Maybe . . . I don't know, I don't buy it. I think we should talk to Farah and see what we can find out about this dealer.

Alright, thinks Johnny, as he and Mia wrap up their conversation and head towards Farah, detectives Soufflé and Goat, on the case. It's a funny occupation, detection. None of this long arm of the law business, naturally, but perhaps the thumb of justice—or . . . was there already a thumb of justice? wouldn't that be more the thumb of injustice, pressing the scales down, ergo, Johnny and Mia, the Counterthumb. Community policing. Policing the community. Doesn't sound great when you say it like that. Ah well. There's a kind of freedom to it, private investigation. Hadn't he had a TA who had said that? Something about social mobility. Seeing all the strata. Lets you quest too. People love to quest. Introduce a little bit of narrative into your life; give it some structure, meaning. But it's the freedom, Johnny thinks, as he and Mia pass again under the archway, emerging into Carneval (which, at this point, is really rocking and rolling; yes, it's gearing up to be one for the ages here; no doubt Johnny is on to something with his catharsis thesis, though calling it that may be a bit reductive: his framework is nothing if not heterodox, drawing heavily from the canonical Steam Valve literature, clearly, but also being deeply informed by the Second World thesis, among others—ever since the Linguini Twins mobilized their ecological critique, things in the field have been . . . well, we could spend all day frolicking in the thorny undergrowth of theoretical minutiae, but it seems that Johnny is on the verge of solving another, or several, of life's great problems, and we don't want to miss this) so if you accept that (oops!) sure, it's obvious: all human thought is flawed. But that doesn't mean we shouldn't do it. It's like this. Everything is made of atoms. Atoms are made of protons, electrons, and neutrons. Protons, electrons, and neutrons are made of, what, quarks? And quarks are made of . . . something. Strings? Whatever. What matters is that something is made of something, which is made of something, which is made of something—it's something all the way down. But let's take the smallest possible thing. Smallest unit of matter. We'll call it LittleAtom. And we'll say that the universe is made up of these LittleAtoms, and that every LittleAtom occupies one place at one time. Now. What happens when you try to say that two LittleAtoms are the same? You can't. One is at one place at one point in time, and the other is at a different place at the same point in time, so the two can't be the same. Except. Except what if we lose some information? What if we forget about the place in time and just look at the commonality between the LittleAtoms? In other words, what if we abstract? Now we're getting somewhere. Now we can take big groups of these LittleAtoms and identify some common features and say that if they share enough of these common features, then these big groups of LittleAtoms are really the same thing. And that's basically thinking. Because language. It's what words do. They abstract. They have to. Pigeonholes. We don't have a word for every LittleAtom, so some words have to do double-duty. Or million-duty. Or whatever. You get the idea. We're trying to describe reality, but reality resists description. So we fail. We take something complete, something real, and we reduce it, warp it, change it into something that we can use. Even the most precise thinkers do this. Everyone does this. It's just how thinking works. Also, don't forget: things change. So we have to think about that. Not only are two LittleAtoms, or LittleAtom conglomerates, not the same, but at different points in time, the same LittleAtom might be different. Shit. This is a lot to keep track of. And we haven't even started to think about what a LittleAtom might be—like, who's to say there's not a LittlerAtom? Or a LittlestAtom? Fuck. FUCK. Okay. Scrap the LittleAtom. Scrap strings and quarks and neutrons and protons and regular atoms and elements and molecules and cells and organelles and organs and bodies and societies and planets and solar systems and galaxies and all the rest— let's think about how there's just one thing. One universe. OneThing. And let's think about how any attempt to break this OneThing up, to separate the universe into this and that— any attempt to think, really—is going to mean failure. In the real world, there is no such thing as a person. There is no such thing as a mountain. There is no such thing as a beer or a cup or an atom. There is just the OneThing. Fuck, is that what god is, Johnny wonders, as he halts to let a particularly long, questionably ironic conga line pass.

— Johnny motherfucking Soufflé! — shouts one of the conga liners.

— Johnny motherfucking Soufflé! — shouts the rest of the conga line.

Johnny gives a cordial wave, but his heart's not in it. He's still thinking. Thinking about thinking. Thinking that it doesn't really matter how you get there, whether you want to go the

LittleAtom route, or whether you want to go the OneThing route, whichever way you go, big or small, you're going to arrive at one conclusion: to try to think completely, to try and wriggle the universe into a complete system of laws and axioms and truths and smaller systems, that's a fool's errand. Never going to work. But it's okay. Because not all of us want to try and think completely. Especially not when it comes to thinking about humans and the societies they create. Most of us know that'll never work. Most of us just want to see results. So here's a way out of the conundrum: if you accept that all human thought is failure, that no abstraction completely covers whatever it's describing, that there's always information lost, that no two things are the same, that everything is changing—if you take all that as axiomatic, then surely the solution to the conundrum is not just to try and create as dynamic a system of thought as possible, one that recognizes failure as its basis, but also, to create a system of thought that creates its own failure. It's not enough for us to recognize that humans and the societies they create are always changing. We have to change them. We have to improve. Be better. *Better*. It's a loaded word. Who gets to define it? After all, how much violence has ridden under the banner of *progress*? Unspeakable amounts, no question. But there's a type of cynic who looks at those who have used *progress* to orchestrate some of the most heinous human suffering imaginable and sees another cynic, sees someone every bit as attuned to the massive gulf between their ideals and their actions as they are. For a certain type of cynic, this is reassuring. It can be difficult to accept that some people really believe; that there are ideas worth dying for, and ideas worth killing for, and that this can be true while it is simultaneously true that all ideas are inevitably broken and incomplete in some fundamental way; that it is in fact this very inevitable brokenness and incompleteness that keeps those loftiest ideas of liberation from returning to their birthplace, that most heinous human suffering imaginable; that making moves in this world, really making moves, having any sort of power and exercising it, means accepting that you are one in a very long line of people that thought they could change the world, and that after you will come an even longer line of people that think they can change the world, and that what you and everyone who came before you and everyone who came after you all share in common is failure, fucking up, forgetting the wisdom of elders, disregarding the complaints of youngers, like everything else in the history of this universe, decaying and dying—all of which is true, of course, unless you are different, somehow: unprecedented, world-historical. There is always the possibility that it is you who will bring humanity out of its troubled adolescence and into a new era of history so radically different from what came before it that it may as well be a new history itself. The truth is that standing where he stands, seeing what he sees, Johnny has absolutely no idea what this new history will look like. He just knows that it will be beautiful; that at every moment in our history, even as human suffering was at its most imaginably heinous point, there was resilience and beauty and creativity in the face of everything that was doing its very best to crush it, and that when humanity moves into young adulthood, that creativity and beauty and resilient spirit will be unleashed in ways so creative and beautiful and free that it physically hurts to think about. Who gets to define better? We do, of course. Because if we don't, they will. Like every other adolescence, humanity's will not end in a single moment. As it, too, faces decay and death, it will struggle to reassert itself. It will do so violently and without conscience. And there is no guarantee that it will lose. It is our responsibility to see that it does. Because that's what this is about, no? Responsibility. That's what it means to do something, anything. To accept responsibility. To embrace that most basic human condition. Failure. So we're back where we started. Or, thinks Johnny, looking around, wait, where are we?

— Mia?

No Mia. No Carneval either. Johnny turns. There it is, a few hundred feet back. He checks his phone. Like seventeen messages and . . .

02:05:12

So that's normal, at least. He's in the neighborhood now. Better not to linger. The rules are different here. He could text Mia. He looks again at his phone, which is emitting a threatening aura. Is that a bump on his screen? No way he's dealing with this now; he's just gonna slide that one back into the pocket and hope for the best.

Once again, Johnny approaches Carneval, observant. They're having fun today. As they should. It's a party. And yet. It's weird, being back. That's what he was trying to explain to Ali. The feeling that you don't belong anymore. Like a tourist. Isn't that what nostalgia is? Tourism of the past. Jeez.

Johnny looks over at one of the lawns, where a blatant disregard for trampoline safety is being offset by some unimpeachably good vibes. And someone's bringing out snacks. What a life.

— Johnny. Motherfucking. Soufflé.

Johnny turns.

— Mike! Love the dress.

Mike twirls around a bit.

— It's got pockets, — he says, coyly.

— It sure does. How you been? Heard you're running The Weekly now.

— Ugh. Don't remind me.

—That bad?

— It's fucked. We're fucked. Everything's fucked. You seen the video?

— No?

Mike pulls his phone out.

— One sec . . . fuck. They took it down again.

— What's the video?

— Someone . . . you just have to see it. It's fucked, Johnny. If it's real. No one knows yet. You here alone?

— I wasn't but . . . took some Tr-Y, got kind of lost.

— Tripping. Gotcha. Definitely don't want to see this video then. You headed somewhere?

— Not really sure.

— Come with me then. I'm headed to TOM. Got a lead there.

— You're working today?

— Something like that.

— Alright. Any chance you've got a lighter in those pockets?

— Sorry.

Johnny makes a noise Mike doesn't seem sure how to interpret. But it's no big deal. The duo weave through the throngs of Carnevalgoers, dodging party projectiles, navigating quick hellos, catching up. They make it to TOM in record time, where Johnny, who has a sixth sense for this kind of thing, manages to intuit this year's homophonic Carneval theme well before he's had a chance to glance at the large banner hanging above the DJ, where a hundred-some lures rattle, unheard; the only thing Johnny can hear is the almost tangibly thick bassline, which, on second thought, might actually just be tangible, and, on third thought, seems less a tangible feature of the room and more somehow woven into the fabric of the room itself, which is flexing with every hit, like the matter's gone convex, bloated by a bassline so powerful that when it stops, like it just did, its absence is enough to send the room into a state of mild implosion, concave now, fishing jackets pulled towards the DJ, who's smiling, like she's seeing it too, her power, this warp. And now it's back, stronger than ever, the room is once again expanding, then contracting, then expanding, muscular, thinks Johnny, as he and Mike snake between the dancers, through the next room, and out onto the patio, where an acceptable number of spliffs are in rotation, and the stories are flowing.

— It was her birthday! So she decides to kill a fifth of

vodka by herself, which, like, bad idea, but I'm not her mom, so whatever, we left the party and then met up with some friends and went home, at which point, it was like, I don't know, 2 or something, and we start smoking and hanging out, and then we get this knock on the door, and it's her sorority sisters, who have basically hauled her up the stairs to our room and then literally dropped her off at the front door, like, *she's really drunk, can you make sure she gets to bed*? but really drunk doesn't even begin to describe it, she's totally unresponsive, like we can't even get her to react to her name, and like I don't know if you've ever had to take care of someone like that, but it's scary, it's like . . . like all the like animating consciousness has been vacated, and you're left with this like flesh puppet, and you really start to think about how we're all just bodies . . . like . . . I don't know, I've never felt so like physical . . . but anyways I was pretty high and so was everyone else, and it's after 2, so the RA is off-duty, but we call her anyways, and she comes up to the room and is like, *no way I'm dealing with this right now*, so she calls 911, and they show up in a few minutes, like a cop and a couple EMTs, and we're obviously high, like I'm pretty sure there was still smoke like in the room, but hey it's legal so whatever, one of the EMTs starts shining a flashlight in her eyes, which starts to wake her up, and slowly she's becoming more and more conscious, and then the EMT asks her who the president is, and she says this name, and it's the fucking president of her sorority! which obviously the EMT doesn't know so he starts to ask her more questions but now she's seeming more and more lucid, and they're like, *okay what have you had to drink*, and she's really feeling herself now like, *sorry officer, it was my birthday, things got a little out of hand, I had four, maybe five drinks,* and now she's totally conscious, and of course they can't take her to the hospital if she doesn't want to go so they end up basically pulling us aside and telling us to make sure she drinks a lot of water and then they leave-

— And that was it?

— No! Because the next thing that happens is she turns to us and is like, *why the FUCK did you call the cops, I had molly in my jacket and I was FINE,* and it's like, no dude, you were literally about to die, and she's like, *I was fine,* and then goes to her room and falls asleep. And that was it. Didn't even thank us the next day.

— Damn.

— I kind of had the opposite thing happen to me today.

— Yeah?

— Yeah. We were in Pinnekjøtt. It was me, Arjun, and Arjun's friend Doogh. Do you know them?

— Don't think so.

— Yeah. Well. They were tripping hard. I think it was Tr-Y. They were on something. And for the first bit we could understand them. They were pretty lucid, but you know, obviously tripping. And then . . . and then they just started babbling? And it's sort of like what you were talking about. Unresponsive. But the opposite. Too much consciousness.

— So what'd you do?

— Arjun kind of just shook them.

— Shook them?

— Not hard! But like, enough. Seemed to work?

— You're Kai?

— Yeah?

— Mike Beef, with The Weekly, we emailed a bit earlier today.

— Oh right, right. Good timing.

— Yeah, we've heard of a few similar incidents. Tr-Y, you said?

— I think so.

— It's his DotB receptors, — volunteers Johnny, as he graciously accepts a traveling spliff.

Mike frowns.

— Don't know about that. Do you happen to know where he got the Tr-Y? We're thinking it's a bad batch.

— Mia thought so too. We saw the same thing happen earlier. We were going to look into it, and then I got sort of . . . lost.

— Uh huh. Kai if you don't mind, I'd like to ask you a few questions.

— Sure.

— Maybe a little privacy, — says Mike, gesturing to a pair of open seats on the lawn.

— Sure.

Kai and Mike depart.

— Anyone have a lighter I could . . . thanks, y'all don't mind if I smoke?

— Go ahead.

This cigarette has seen better days. But soon it'll be ash. Ash on the patio.

— So, Mike mentioned something about a video? — Johnny
says, to no one in particular.

— Don't know anything about that.

Another spliff arrives at Johnny. He sidelines the cigarette
and takes an ambitious hit.

— Might want to be careful there.

Exhaling,

— Why's that?

— That's THC Kush.

— Oh?

— And there's kief.

— Right on.

Everyone's quiet again. You can still hear the bass, bump-
ing. Something seems off. Johnny's not quite sure what.

The door to the patio opens again,

— . . . and now she's being hounded by all these ghoul-
ish right-wing media goyim because of that Reviewed article
about her.

— No shit.

— Yeah it's disgusting. Imagine being paid that much and
still being so fragile that you're worried about a twenty-year-
old's op-ed. Unreal.

Turning to the smoking circle,

— Oh. Hey.

— You're talking about that op-ed?

— The drama never stops.

Turning to Johnny,

— You look familiar. Have we met?

— Don't think so. Johnny.

— Leah. Nice to meet you. Do you live in TOM?

— Graduated last year.

— And you're back? — says one of the circle, looking up from a half-rolled spliff, — I'm getting the fuck out of here, man, and I'm never looking back.

— Same.   — Same.   — Same.

Johnny nods, with empathy.

— So why are you here?

— Just seeing some friends.

— Hold on, — says another one of the circle, — I thought I recognized you. You're that Johnny, aren't you? the one everyone's always talking about.

— Holy shit! No way. In the flesh.

Johnny smiles with what seems like the right amount of gap-toothed demure.

— Legend.

— Is it true you-

— Sorry to interrupt, — says an alarmed-looking Leah, — but does that drone belong to any of you?

Johnny and the circle follow her finger to a small drone floating in front of the trees, although it's a little far for Johnny's eyes, especially given their current drug regimen.

— Not mine.

— Mine either.

— What's it doing?

— It's definitely facing us.

— That light's blinking.

— A camera?

— We could throw something at it.

— Doesn't Jermaine have a drone like that?

— Fuck if I know.

—We could definitely throw something at it.

— I don't want to break his shit.

— I don't think it's his, — says one of the circle, looking up from her phone, — Jermaine's off-campus right now.

— You track him too?

— I track all my friends.

— There's a volleyball down there.

— That'll work.

— Johnnyboy.

Down the patio stairs, maybe a foot away from where Mike and Kai are sitting, there's a volleyball lying in the grass. Johnny starts to move towards it. The drone tracks him.

— Woah.

— Spooky.

— Johnny come back.

Johnny returns. The drone tracks him again.

— Now back again.

Johnny goes back towards the volleyball. The drone tracks him, waits a second, and then leaves.

— What in the actual fuck?

— That's what I'm saying, man. This place is fucked.

— Probably just some bored freshman.

— Maybe they're making a movie.

— About Johnny?

— About Carneval.

— Maybe.

— Hey Johnny you good? You look . . .

— Yeah, — says Johnny, — just a little . . . high.

— Legend.

Everyone laughs.

— I think I'm going to head out, — Johnny says, as he calls out to Mike, walks back inside, goes past the DJ, opens the door, steps out onto the front lawn, and assesses his situation—vibe check: he's catastrophically high.

02:20:38

And he's not even three hours in. Fuck. Maybe he should hit up Mia for some Pr-X. See if he can come down a bit. To Iremia, then.

Johnny heads that way. He's pretty fucked up. Babaganoushed, honestly. And the job—fuck! Johnny's forgotten all about the natch pulse. He considers the phone in his pocket. Maybe he has a message from The Office of the President: yes, as a matter of fact, our drone has been tracking you, from the payphone to the frat to Iremia to The Institute to the neighborhood to TOM and now here, into the midst of Carneval; we're very upset: you have not been doing your job. But but but, Johnny protests, hasn't he been doing exactly what he's supposed to be doing? Observing. Ruminating. Living in the grips of radical authenticity. It's just a matter of whipping up a report, which he can do easily. No. Forget that. It wasn't The Office of the President's drone. There are always drones flying around this campus. Some bored freshman. Everything's fine. He breathes. So why is everyone looking at him? Is there something on his face? Doesn't feel like there's anything— fuck! His mask. Probably left it at The Institute. Maybe Mia will have a spare. It's fine. No cause for concern. He can relax. The masks are a cute idea. Level the playing field. Useful, too. Sometimes you need to be someone else to be yourself. Of course, you're always yourself. But sometimes you're less yourself. And sometimes you're more yourself. It ebbs. It flows. It's porous, your self. No one's an atom. Light needs dark, dark needs light. So it is with people. No Mia without Johnny, no Johnny without Mia. For people, for culture, for things, for places—everything in relation. Relation. Relation. (Here Johnny's thoughts melt into something more or less supralinguistic, the kind of soupy, narcotheoretical inquiry that even we are having some difficulty making sense of. Suffice to say, when his thoughts emerge from the oils, solid again, things are still a bit shaky.) Carneval. Again. Party. Good. God. He's blitzed. These abstractions. They're peeling off the earth. He can see them. Skeletal. Huh. That looks like Sarah. Check out her gender. Powerful stuff. More abstractions. God he's zooted. The Tr-Y. The weed. A little nicotine. It's synergetic. Synergistic? Synergized. That's right. Synthesis. Fuck! Why's the ground all . . . bloody? Eyes closed. Ouch. Sorry. Sorry! My bad. Shake it off. No more blood, at least. Deep breaths. Take it all in. Sun, shining. Breeze, breezing. Festivities, festivating. Deep breaths. He's fine. Everything's fine. It's a beautiful day. Tomorrow he'll wake up, he'll write a report, and he'll watch as thousands of dollars of debt disappear. He'll return to his life in the city, where he's paid, where things are good. It's fine. Everything's fine. He can feel himself returning to normal. The visuals are already waning. He can think again. He looks around. He's here, isn't he? That's what matters. He's here. He's here! Alive. Oh god. Shouldn't have opened that door. But there's no stopping it now. Here they come. The things he used to feel, things no one should have to feel. And yet. If he hadn't felt those things, how could he feel what he's feeling right now? This joy. The one that's auxiliary to the love. The joy of being here. Maybe this is the kind of joy only the formerly suicidal know. Their private joy. The kind you can't explain to other people without first explaining what it feels like to really, truly, without qualification, want to die. What it feels like to live with that poison in your head, day-in, day-out. These are not the things you want to explain to other people. Many will not understand. At best, they will worry about you. They will feel a compassion that you appreciate but cannot understand. A stranger's compassion. But you would understand. God. You did understand. Which isn't what you told his family. Or your family. Or any of your friends. But you got it. You understood. Not that that made it hurt any less. Maybe it made it hurt more. You don't know. What you do know is that you're here, now. You're alive. And you're you. There is little-to-nothing universal to the trans experience, but this should be: the love you feel for your self. All of it, in all of its mess: its imperfections, its failures, its limitations, its impossibilities. You love it. You're Johnny Soufflé. And there's joy in that. Because there's joy in life. There is. So, as Johnny approaches Iremia, he smiles. He's here. He's here.

Someone else is entering Iremia. Johnny falls in line behind them, snagging the door, and finding himself once again faced with the kitchen. It's a riot of smells in there, but Johnny's not going to linger, and neither will we—instead we'll follow him right up the stairs, and outside of Mia's room, where he pauses to collect his breath and steady himself.

The door is slightly open. Johnny can hear Mia's voice:

— I don't know! I lost him when we were walking through Carneval and he's not answering his phone.

Well that's-

— Weird, — says a voice that sounds a lot like Priya.

— It's fine. They just said to make sure he takes the Tr-Y they gave me and to have him talk with Rachele. And we did that.

— Do you think I should've-

— No, you were great. I think it's fine. I just want to know that he's safe . . . hey don't give me that look.

— If you wanted him to be safe-

— It's all my loans!

A beat.

— You're right, you're right.

— Besides, it's not like he was going to be here sober.

— You think?

Mia snorts,

— If I know Johnny motherfucking Soufflé.

Another beat.

— Still can't believe everyone calls him that.

— Yeah, — says Mia, sighing, — you'd think he'd have realized by now.

— Yeah, — says Priya, thoughtfully, as Johnny backs away from the door, back down the stairs, through the kitchen, and out to the front door, where the overwhelming sight of Carneval forces him to flee into the back streets.

What the fuck? Whatthefuck, whatthefuck, whatthefuck? He's tripping. Right? He's tripping. He should go back. Go back to Mia and ask her from some Pr-X. Wait until he comes down. Then he can talk to her. Figure out whatever he needs to figure out. God. What the fuck? The contract. The Tr-Y. The drone. It's all-

His phone buzzes.

Yeah fucking right.

His phone buzzes.

If it's The Office of the President.

His phone buzzes.

Johnny looks. It's River. He hangs up. Sorry River. Not right now. He needs to go somewhere quiet. Sort through this. Somebody's scheming. The contract. The Tr-Y. The drone. Mia. The Office of the President. Rachele. The Hege-M. It's all-

His phone buzzes.

River again?

—River, hey . . . yeah, I'm on campus, what's up? . . . no . . . no, it's not that, I'm just tripping . . . right . . . right . . . no yeah . . . yeah . . . The Tavern? . . . yeah, how long are you going to be there? . . . yeah I could swing by in a bit . . . yeah, — laughs, — no yeah . . . okay . . . I'll see you soon.

He hangs up and looks at his phone. He's got a lot of messages. A few missed calls from Mia. One from River. He speeds through the messages. They're all from friends. Heard he's on campus. Want to see him, if he has the time. Nothing from The Office of the President.

02:31:29

Johnny looks around. No drones, as far as he can see. He looks back at Iremia. Maybe he is just tripping. Who knows what he heard? He is on Drugs. No. No no no. Something's up. The contract. The Tr-Y. The drone. Mia. The Office of the President. Rachele. The Hege-M. It's all connected, somehow. Something's going on.

Johnny watches as a couple approaches one of the neighboring houses, one walking a bike, the other dawdling alongside.

Here are the facts: he's been brought to the University campus to attend Carneval and produce a report on the student body; he's been given free Drugs; someone was—is?—watching him. Someone is also flooding University with bad Tr-Y. Bad, but essentially harmless, right? Hege-M or whatever. It's harmless. And even if he's being watched, even if he's being manipulated, what danger is he in?

The couple lock the bike to a crowded rack and enter the house.

Not much? No police at Carneval. Thank the organizers for that. There do seem to be shadowy, conspiratorial forces, but maybe the best thing for him to do is exactly what he would normally do, were he on Drugs, at a giant party, with a bunch of his friends. Who knows what these forces'll do if they think he's onto them?

Better to play it safe, then. River wants him to swing by The Tavern? He'll swing by The Tavern. Food could be good. Though he's not very hungry. Never is, when he's tripping.

But it'd be nice to see River. He'll head that way.

Johnny starts to stroll towards The Tavern, his mind awash. The walk there can't be more than five, maybe six minutes; nevertheless, for those in the throes of Tr-Y, it's enough. To get to The Tavern, Johnny first has to walk through Watercress, the small commercial center in the middle of campus, where there's a few restaurants, a bike shop, some other stuff, and, today, a number of people, living their lives, something which is presently giving Johnny the strong sensation that he is at the zoo, though whether he is one of the animals or the one watching them is still an open question. And by the time Johnny's arrived at the courtyard outside of The Tavern, he's no closer to closing it.

He decided to take a bit of a circuitous path, so he arrives at the back of the courtyard unnoticed, giving him more than a few seconds to take it all in, life in the courtyard: dozens of people, each wearing a full-head plastic mask, all the same: same bloodshot eyes, same eccentric freckles, same gap-toothed smile—and with their matching outfits, the bounty of jorts, dirty flannels, thrift store tees, and, yes, bucket hats, there's really no question about what's going on here: this courtyard's full of Soufflés: Soufflés lounging; Soufflés standing; Soufflés cross-legged; Soufflés full spread; Soufflés on their phones; Soufflés talking with one another, deheaded, angling beer down their throats; here's a Soufflé in the midst of a coughing attack, receiving nothing but callous laughter from her cronies, who are hitting the vape pen with careless abandon, just, it seems, to flex; here's a second Soufflé, only a few feet behind, sneaking garlic-studded fries off an abandoned plate; there's a third Soufflé, pointing at the fry scavenger and saying something presently being ignored by fourth and fifth Soufflés, who seem to have gotten in some sort of dispute, poor Soufflé six caught in the middle, trying to make peace; everywhere he looks there's a new Soufflé, and look at that: here's one headed right his way.

— Johnny. Mother. Fucking. Sou. Fflé, — says the approaching Soufflé, removing their mask to reveal the familiar face of River Juice. — What do you think? It's The Afternoon Of A Hundred Johnnys.

But before Johnny can respond, the other Soufflés realize what's going on, and—in unison—they chant:

— Johnny! Mother! Fucking! Sou! Fflé! Johnny! Mother! Fucking! Sou! Fflé!

What would you do? Johnny gives River a hug, mentions something about being far too high to deal with this right now, and hauls ass down the nearest road. Now then. Let's hop out of the parentheticals and get serious for a second. Being bipolar, Johnny has experienced his fair share of delusions. If you haven't, you may not know what it feels like to have your reality crumple. It's not fun. For the curious, there are drugs that might artificially recreate this experience. But because if you do this, you will achieve your delusions artificially, in a time and place of your choosing, it might become difficult to recreate the full experience. If you're anything like us, it's the lack of trust that gets you. It gnaws at you, this feeling. Let's call it reality insecurity. The feeling that at any moment, the rug may be pulled out from underneath you, and everything you think in that moment, everything that feels so real and true, will turn out to be wrong. Deluded. It's true that sometimes this can be a relief. If your delusion is one of worthlessness, for example, you might be comforted to know that you have worth, that your life is worth living. But still. It gnaws at you. Which brings us to Johnny here. As he was hauling ass down the nearest road, we took a look into his head; what we found was not pretty. He's hurting. Hurting bad. Seeing all those Soufflés broke something inside of Johnny. He no longer feels in control; the world feels hostile; he wants to go home. He feels insane. Reality has gotten away from him. The effects of nicotine combined with Tr-Y are well known, but little research has been done on the effects of Tr-Y and marijuana on the bipolar brain; nevertheless, an influential case study by Momo, Fattoush, Water, and Genoise has shown that certain psychedelic drugs have the potential to trigger psychotic episodes; for this reason, bipolar people are often cautioned away from psychedelic use, Johnny included. The problem is that Johnny loves psychedelics. Loves drugs, really. He believes in them: believes that approached with the right mindset, under the right conditions, drugs can be a valuable part of someone's life. More to the point, Johnny thinks that drugs have been a valuable part of his life. They are a point of pride for Johnny, something he thinks he's good at. He is currently being humbled; you probably know what that feels like—we certainly do. It hurts, and right now, Johnny does not feel that he is particularly good at doing drugs. He does not feel that he is particularly good at being bipolar. And if you want the honest truth, as he thoughtlessly runs towards a certain West Campus parking lot, sinking, Johnny does not feel that he's particularly good at being alive. It has been years since Johnny has thought seriously about suicide. You can imagine how much it hurts to find himself thinking about it again. One consequence of dysphoria-forward trans narratives is that the time before transition is widely understood to be, psychically speaking, wretched; add in a bipolar diagnosis, something which Johnny is not particularly coy about, and you'll find that no one is much surprised that Johnny has the capacity to feel great pain. It's something people seem to immediately pick up on, despite his generally positive and upbeat vibe; even among his acquaintances, it's more or less understood that if he is generally positive and upbeat, it's because he's been so sad and in pain that he never wants to feel that way again. The people in Johnny's life tend to find this pat explanation endearing; those of us who knew him at University certainly did. He is loved. But it's a complicated love, and right now, Johnny does not feel it; he feels alone. He's just made it to that West Campus parking lot, where he is, in fact, alone, not a soul in sight. He stops to breathe. Several snappa tables have been abandoned and left uncleaned; cases of beer sit askew in the grass like broken tombstones. Johnny grimaces. The entitlement. The presumption that their mess will be cleaned up. He's remembering an old roommate now, one who had spoken often, and with fervor, about the largely invisible labor force without which University would cease to function; maybe, posited the old roommate, you had to have yourself once been largely invisible to understand; maybe you had to have been marginal; it's like these people had only ever moved through society with the absolute conviction that it was for them, the old roommate had said—and why shouldn't they, thinks Johnny now: it is: the rapists win; the war criminals get tenure; the robber barons get eponymous buildings and their children get to study in them—there's nothing broken about the system; it works; it works well. And now he's in despair. He's just considered the system. It crushed him. We're fucked, he thinks. We'd give him the mic back, but that characteristic Soufflé reversal won't come. Things have just gotten worse. Johnny has just realized where he is, and looking away from the snappa tables, back towards the parking lot, he sees no payphone; it's been removed. Johnny freaks. He runs away from the West Campus parking lot and goes straight to the steps leading up to Lake Bog; he climbs them and is now overlooking the lake: to his left, a path leading to the outskirts of Carneval; to his right, a path that goes into the woods.

— Johnnnnnnnnnny.

Johnny looks around.

— Johnnnnnnnnnnny Soufflèèè.

Johnny looks around. No one's there.

— Johnny, it's the Trees. Come sit with us; sit with us and listen to our tale.

So:

The Tale of the Trees

We begin with a boy, not quite a man, and a sandwich, not quite complete. Let us set the scene: it is late; it is Tuesday; in another world, it is an hour reserved for witching, but here it is the purview of procrastinators and the depraved: with one twenty-four-hour exception, the libraries have closed for the night, funneling a series of all-nighters outwards, some to their singles, others to the common spaces, a few to the dining halls, which are already teeming: stoners peruse containers of leftovers, riffs endless, laughter joyous, homemade sauces questionable, if, in a pinch, hitting. They move in crews; in this particular dining hall, there are two: a trio and a quartet, the former parked in front of the microwave, the latter already seated at one of the tables, both eyeing the other's snacks—a beautiful friendship is about to be born.

But that is only the second most important thing that will happen tonight. The first concerns one of the library exiles, who loiters outside the dining hall, polishing off the last of a hastily rolled joint. He is thinking about space. Ah, the universe! So big and full of things. Like many in search of a science credit, our hero has ended up in an introductory astrophysics class, one whose demands, presently exerted, are more existential than mathematical, requiring its students contemplate things like the humble neutron star, a spoonful of which weighs enough -illions of tons to send even the soberest of budding scientists into a fit of psychic distress. But with an exhale, and a stub, our hero manages to move on, through the door, past the septet now gathered around a plate of chicken nuggets and what appears to be honey mustard, onto the fridge, where lunch's leftover sandwich ingredients can be found.

There are other foods, too, but something a little more than kismet and not quite providence guides a pair of glassy eyes to the lone loaf on the counter. He slices and then opens the refrigerator door, exposing a large plastic wrap dome, whose walls are sure to fall, soon, when our hero settles on a plan of attack. Turkey? Ham? Not quite. He unpeels a few slices of roast beef, shingling them onto the bottom bread. Cheese time. Cheddar. Sharp? There's only one kind. This, too, is shingled. Now for texture and twang. A handful of arugula. The pickled onions in the back of the fridge, which glow, helpfully. Sauce: a seemingly obscene amount of horseradish. He likes his sinuses clear. Slather that on. It's assembled; he's ready to bite.

This was the first Moment. The second would happen many years later, in his first, and only, formal interview.

"Have you always had this gift?"

"No."

"So you wouldn't consider yourself something of a savant?"

"No."

"Then surely you must have gone through some sort of rigorous training?"

"No."

"A mentor?"

"No."

The interviewer paused.

"So," she said, "you do not consider yourself a genius."

"No."

"Do you consider yourself an exceptionally hard worker?"

"No."

The interviewer paused once more.

"So you mean to tell me that the world's foremost artist, an artist whose critical and commercial success is, to put it bluntly, unrivaled, someone who has taken their creative field, elevated it, destroyed it, built it back again, that this artist, you, can credit neither talent nor ethic for your success? What, then," she asked "could possibly explain it?"

The Sandwich Artist pondered this.

"I'm not really sure," he said, finally.

"You can't even begin to explain."

"No," he said, "I'm not really sure it's success."

And then he unclipped his mic, stood up from his chair, and walked out of the studio.

So began the second phase. The first, of course, began that night: a sandwich, completed; a man, all grown up. He dropped out of University expeditiously, finding employment in the nearest sandwich joint. Shortly fired on account of some unlicensed late-night experimentation, he quickly found employment in the second-nearest sandwich joint. The rest of the trajectory is well known and predictable: a few months of perfect, albeit restrained, execution, followed by the manager's discovery of his talents; the auditioning of an initial sandwich; the nigh-orgasmic reception therein; the discovery of a secondary, literary talent (sandwich-naming); and then, within a few more months, a near-total rehaul of the menu; lines around the block; a review in the local paper; another, picked up, one day, by the nearby city's resident sandwich critic, who made the journey down for another nigh-orgasmic reception; a job offer; a move; lines around the block; a review in the national paper; an attempted profile (rejected); a requested interview (rejected); government funding (accepted); the training and appointing of a second-in-command, who handled day-to-day operations as The Sandwich Artist pursued more experimental craft at the recently founded Institute for Sandwich Studies; another attempted profile (rejected); a global tour; the invention, and widespread success, of sandwich diplomacy; a retreat from the public eye; a renewed focus on the art; a civil union; an adoption; family life (strained); philanthropic efforts; a second, more intensely renewed focus on the art; an interview (accepted); and then, as previously discussed, phase two.

What is a sandwich? That was the question at the front of The Sandwich Artist's mind. Deconstruction proved swift and ruthless; alas, critical reception was mixed: perverse intellectual pleasures are short-lived; his "readymades" felt more like a stunt than a serious engagement with the tradition. The critics longed for a return to the substantial subs of days past, but those days were, indeed, past: at home, things festered; in the studio, they blossomed. It was a period of verdant creativity for The Sandwich Artist. Who eats a sandwich? That was the second question he considered. Was it an abstraction he cooked for, or a real person? Consider materiality and politics are sure to follow. So it was with The Sandwich Artist, whose Revolutionary Turn can be divided into two neat periods: utopian and not. The less said about these periods, the better. Three years went by; nothing changed. The Sandwich Artist, defeated, regressed. He returned to his second question. What is the relationship between artist, sandwich, and eater? Conventional wisdom saw it bifurcated: artist creates sandwich; eater eats sandwich—there seemed to be a disconnect, a rupture in the social relation. He began to consider taste. What was it that he looked for in a sandwich? A level of craftsmanship, to be sure, but more to the point, a level of consciousness. Wasn't that, after all, what eating a truly great sandwich was about? How many sandwiches had he eaten—how many sandwiches had he made—that were technically perfect and utterly dead? (Johnny murmurs). Precisely, Johnny. Life. Good sandwiches illuminate chains; great sandwiches rattle them. And ever the rattler, The Sandwich Artist continued down his arcane path. What, really, did it mean for something to be edible? What would it mean for a sandwich to reject its most basic assumption: that it can be eaten? He began to experiment. A cloth wrap, a tire sub, sand in the sauce. The culture had caught up to him: critics raved, but The Sandwich Artist bemoaned. Yes, the inedible was disorienting, but it quickly became an object of removed contemplation. An abstraction. Dead. It was all struggle, no reward. So he played with form factor: delicious sandwiches that nevertheless pushed up against all manner of mandibular restraint. Too wide. Too tall. Too heavy. No doubt you see where this is headed. A sandwich that gave you hives. A sandwich that made you hallucinate. A sandwich that left you, quite literally, empty. A sandwich that gave you chills. Finally, in this world of drugs and poisons, The Sandwich Artist had found what he was looking for. A sandwich you would never forget. A sandwich you could struggle with. A sandwich that reminded you what it felt like to be alive.

Humans often conceive of suicide as failure. When they found The Sandwich Artist on the floor of his studio, very much dead, intention was assumed; his poison experiments were well known, but so, of course, was his precision. It was not his skill that failed him but his will, said the critics, said the fans, said his partner, said his son, who hated his father, hated his success, hated his art, hated everything about him, even and especially his alma mater, University, a school this son attended, resentfully, for he hated legacy admissions, hated the obscene concentration of wealth, the inequality rampant in the student body, the ongoing mental health crisis—he hated it all, this son of privilege. Oh, how he ached for a better world! Why should the good suffer? Why should the bad be blessed? A world born of random chaos, and ruled by unrepentant evil. So he began to plot and scheme. The transitional nature of a four-year University term meant that every activist came with an expiration date—but what if it didn't? What if he kept a low profile, stuck around, embedded himself in the University machine, destroyed it from within, a saboteur, a cancer? And so he did. And so he has. It's already begun, Johnny. It's already begun. Go to The Grand Feast. There you will find what you are looking for. Until next time . . .

Well what the actual fuck, thinks Johnny, as he stands up, brushes some dirt off his pants, and checks his phone.

06:33:14

Of course, he thinks, looking around. He feels astonishingly sober, his head strangely empty. The peak of a hallucinogenic bender so often expanding the brain in unforeseeable ways, post-peak one tends to experience something akin to being at the beach after high tide, the high water mark still visible in the sand, the waves lapping in its shadow, an image Johnny has struggled to explain after trips past, but rest assured, the incommunicability of mental phenomena is not at the top of his mind right now. He's realized he hasn't had anything to eat since that pastry and, in an act of flagrant disrespect to tripper hygiene, hasn't had anything to drink since that cappuccino. Right now he feels somewhere between clammy and waxy; his skin is like a wet crayon. Things are not looking good.

The Grand Feast. There there would be food, drink, and, if you believe The Trees, something of ominous narrative importance. Here, a rational actor, tuned in to the various cosmic signals being sent their way, might resist the temptation of free food and drink. You would think, then, that the apparently lucid Johnny would not ignore the series of ominously important narrative somethings he has already encountered today. And, indeed, he hasn't. But some habits die hard, and having run all the factors through an opaque calculus we can't begin to reverse engineer, he's made a decision: he's going to that feast.

He's a man on a mission, that much we can tell you. A renewed sense of purpose animates his step as he emerges out from the wilderness, onto the path surrounding the lake. Past the now-crumbling circle of freshmen smoking by the benches, joggers run, obliviously; just above the trees, a soon-to-be-setting sun blazes in the sky. It is the Carneval lull: what's left of the darties smolder on as Carnevalgoers retreat to their dorms, their dining halls, wherever they need to go to rest up for the night ahead, when they will reemerge, and the parties will begin. A squadron of athletes—dressed, it seems, as athletes—greets Johnny as he exits the lake path, enters the street, walks past his old freshman dorm, and returns to the Row.

Iremia's there. He looks up at the window where Mia's room should be. He remembers being outside her room, hearing something, and fleeing. But what exactly did he hear? Feeling considerably more sober than he did lingering outside her door, and with a significant chunk of his recent memory wiped out by the intricacies of sandwich artistry, what he can remember of the conversation becomes the easy target of doubt. How plausible was it, really, that Mia would drug him on orders from the University administration? How plausible was it that the University administration would drug him at all? And why would they want him to talk to Rachele? That would mean that the University administration *expected* there to be Hege-M—and how did Priya factor in? Mike Beef? The drone? The missing payphone? It all felt impossibly convoluted. Here was a simpler explanation: he's on Drugs, and whatever loose constellation of paranoid significance he's assembled over the past . . .

06:40:10

. . . was just that: loose. Yes, there was Hege-M in the Tr-Y, but there are a million and one reasons why wholesale drug dealers may be cutting their drugs. Here's what he would do: he would go to The Grand Feast, he would find something to drink, find something to eat, then he'd go find Mia, explain what had happened, and confirm that nothing untoward was afoot. They'd laugh, swap trip stories, and then he'd go home, sleep, wake up, make up some bullshit for this report, and be on his merry, debt-free way.

Easy. He begins to walk up the hill to Palma; to his right, a king and a clown flirt over a bike; to his left, a couple—costume clearly linked, but nevertheless indecipherable—appear to be fighting. Oof: she just hurled that yogurt container full of water. And now he's crying. Brutal. But the situation seems in control.

Whispers of psychedelia haunt the outer reaches of Johnny's vision as he makes it to the top of the hill; he waves to the trio working security and enters into Palma. The Grand Feast will take place in the backyard, but it would be uncouth for someone like Johnny—who has contributed nothing, save his presence—to eat first. He has his sights set on a large second floor balcony, which overlooks the backyard, giving Johnny a chance to scope it out and, if he's lucky, bum a cigarette.

He's in luck, and look at that, our boy is learning: he even remembers to ask for a lighter.

— Thanks, — he says to his generous benefactor, a short woman in a pig onesie, tits cut out, strapon dangling.

— For Johnny motherfucking Soufflé, anything.

— Right on, — he says, coolly.

Something else has started to percolate through the honeycomb of his consciousness. *Motherfucking. Motherfucking. Motherfucking.* Pensive, he inhales. Below, The Grand Feast: the soup boys he saw in Iremia are back, their veritable cauldron of steaming broth precariously dancing through tonight's arrangements: the pyramid of breads; the salads; the assortment of different co-op slops, mashes, and gruels; a massive tray of tempeh nuggets; and good lord, the jars! which have their own table, a great glass city: wide, tall, smooth, textured, these testaments to thrift and principles of reuse will soon be filled with juices, punches, cocktails, mocktails, wines, beers, EANABs, perhaps the very steaming broth whose vat the soup boys have now managed to deposit onto the far table, relief palpable. *You'd think he'd have realized by now.* Johnny inhales again. Was he a joke? Was that what Mia meant? Could people be that . . . cruel? To laugh at him, behind his back. Humor him. Fuel the delusion. (Another inhale.) No. There was no way. Probably, like everything else in life, it was gray. People liked him. They disliked him. They had fun hanging out with him, but thought he was a bit much. Whatever. He looks down again. Having relieved themselves of their soupy burden, the boys once again emerge from Palma, this time carrying a body. Much to Johnny's relief, it's been beheaded; much to his disgust, it's been skinned. Because it is kind of just fucking disgusting, he thinks, as they hoist the body onto the spit: the way we eat people. It's not like we have to. There are people out there who think it's stupid, who think we could do something, anything, else. And the fact that these dissenters exist is enough to hold everyone else accountable. History will be merciless in its judgments, and the future people of this earth—if there are future people of this earth—will look back in disgust. (Another inhale.) It's true. We're a disgusting species. A violent one. No other species on earth eats its own like we do. Take any period in the history of human civilization, and yes, you might see resilience, you might see creativity, you might see pockets of love, but mostly you'll just see violence. You will see exploitation; you will see rape; you will see carnivores; and you will see cannibals. And you will be disgusted. Because it's disgusting. It's a disgusting world we live in. And everyone knows it. (Another inhale.) Everyone knows it could be better. Oh, but that's too radical! In the *real* world- in the real world a relatively small handful of white people managed to enslave, colonize, and genocide an obscene percentage of the earth's population, a world-historical process that, all signs seem to suggest, will culminate in a global apocalypse—if that isn't sufficiently radical, nothing will be. Johnny finishes his cigarette and stares out at The Grand Feast below, which, he's noticing, is an orgy of blood, seeping out of the ground, and bodies, which are apparently blossoming out of every single object he can see; the conch has been blown, people have started to eat, and it's as if he can see every orifice, gaping, meat entering flesh, bodies entering bodies, an actual orgy now, sucking, fucking, fisting, ropes of cum glazing the batards, shrieks, moans, and now eating again, he can hear everything, the crunches and chews, the guzzling, the gristle, all drowned out by the omnipresent crackle of human flesh roasting on the spit— so he's hallucinating; whatever; he is totally, utterly unfazed. Because what Johnny is feeling right now is more than disgust for his fellow humans, and for life itself: Johnny is feeling the hate. Cruel. That's the word that comes to mind. It is too easy to think that no one is enjoying this. What else could possibly explain it? And what else could possibly explain the cruelty that we extend to each other save, perhaps, the cruelty of the situation we find ourselves in: aware that we exist, and that one day-

— Johnny!

Johnny turns, but says nothing, his face betraying him.

— Sorry, sorry, are you busy?

A gesture that says very little.

— Ah, well, it'll only be a second. I know you probably don't remember me because we only hung out that one time, but I just . . . I just wanted to say thank you I guess. Sorry, I'm on a bunch of Tr-Y right now so I don't know if this is going to make any sense but when we hung out last year and you said that thing about how you're either using gender or gender is using you, you changed my whole life, like for real, you really did, like UGH I just started thinking about like being trans and using gender and what kind of woman I wanted to be, and like I know that you're supposed to be proud to be trans or whatever, but I hated it, I fucking hated it, I really did, like I was so MAD and bitter that I had been born this way, and all I could think about was how easy my life would be if I was cis, and how they don't even know, they just walk around living their little cis lives like totally unaware that they could be anything else, and I was mad, I was so mad, and then we hung out and you said that thing about using gender, and it just clicked for me, I don't know, something clicked, and I realized how fucking beautiful being trans is like it's just so UGH like I'd just been trying to approximate this idea of cis womanhood that I'll just literally never be able to attain and driving myself crazy and being so MAD and bitter and then you said that thing about using gender, and it just clicked for me, like PRIDE, like genuine pride, like this thing that's been so corporatized and hollowed out and made just totally fucking meaningless is actually the most beautiful gay feeling in the whole fucking world and if you think that all being trans is is just trying to be a different cis gender then you're going to go crazy and you're going to be mad and you're going to miss out on this beautiful fucking feeling which is just like this like THING that you realize when you like put on your hot little outfit and you feel hot, like really actually HOT, and you think about how you never got to feel that way and you spent your whole life sad and depressed and everything fucking else and you think wow I can't believe cis people have always got to feel like this but then you realize that cis people NEVER get to feel like this because what you're feeling is trans it's so like TRANS and it's just like ugh like it's so fucking BEAU-TIFUL, like yeah it sucks and it's sad and it's hard and people hate us and want to wipe us off the face of the earth, but none of that is like about being trans you know, not really, it's about being trans in this fucked up cis society and we can change that society, like we can, and we will, because we're going to win, we're going to fucking win.

Johnny blinks.

Someone below screams.

Johnny turns.

— The . . . holy shit . . . the . . . — she says, pointing at her phone.

The person seated next to her glances over her shoulder.

— Oh what the fuck.

— What?　　　— What?　　　— What?　　　— What?

— What?　　　— What?　　　— What?　　　— What?

— The QuadSquad, — she manages, — check your email.

A ripple of checked phones moves through the crowd.

— Holy shit! She's . . .

— On fire.

— Fuck.

— Holy shit.

Everyone's watching the video now. Johnny, who, since graduating, is no longer on the QuadSquad mailing list, nevertheless manages to glance at his roof partner's phone. Holy shit, he thinks.

Below: pandemonium. People are yelling, crying, throwing shit; someone just puked.

The sound of the conch cuts through the air. Next to the conch blower, someone is standing by the sound system, holding a mic.

— STOP! Everyone stop.

Everyone stops.

— Thank you. Okay. Everyone just take a deep breath. What we just saw was highkey fucked up. Traumatic, even. And I want to respect that. But we need to keep our shit together. I know a lot of folks are on Tr-Y right now, but we have Pr-X, which Cindy just went to find. We'll make sure everyone gets it. But please, everyone, just sit tight. We can process this together.

Murmurs throughout the crowd.

— Does anyone know her name?

— We should have a vigil. In the Main Quad.

— We can start a fund for her family.

— We should fucking riot, — says a boy standing near the back of the feast.

— Sit down, Chip, — says the girl from earlier.

— We should. We should go to Main Quad, and we should burn this shit to the ground.

— Yeah? You want to burn down your dad's building? — says someone in the crowd.

A deep red grabs hold of Chip's face.

— Fuck you.

— Sit down, Chip, — Leah whispers.

— No, fuck that. And fuck all of you. A girl sets herself on fucking fire and you want to *process*? This isn't about you. This isn't about your feelings. Someone is dead. Get that through your heads. Her life is gone. And you want to process. Fuck you. Everyone here likes to act like they're this big fucking radical because they know a few words and have shitty tattoos. Well I'm fucking tired of it. This is bullshit. If anyone wants to do something about this, you can fucking find me. Fuck you, — he says, giving everyone the finger, and storming off.

No one says anything.

— Well that's uh, — says the emcee, — here's Cindy. If you need Pr-X, talk to her. Not everyone at once though. Everyone else, um . . .

Meanwhile, our boy Johnny is up on the roof, losing it. The Trees were right. The Trees were fucking right! All the threads spinning together and disintegrating. That Pr-X cannot come fast enough.

— The group chat's blowing up. They all saw it.

— Okay.

— They're saying we should march on Main Quad.

— Fuck me man.
— Yeah.
— Fuck.   — Fuck.   — Fuck.   — Fuck.
— Fuck.   — Fuck.   — Fuck.   — Fuck.
— Yeah.
— Is everyone getting their Pr-X?

Drug fairies move through the crowd, distributing tabs of Pr-X; the sun sets in the sky. Things are looking mighty crepuscular, and perhaps the transitional nature of things is on everyone's mind as the Tr-Y ebbs and wanes, synapses taking a much-needed break as a thousand thought processes come to a close. Someone on the roof has managed to get some Pr-X down Johnny's throat, along with some water and a little bit of bread; now he's coming to, just in time to witness the slow migration of people out from the garden below down to the streets, where they'll return to their dorms, change out of the costumes that now seem frivolous and gauche, into their marching clothes. Markers are being grabbed; the University supply of unused cardboard is being rapidly depleted; campus is alive. Those formerly intoxicated have all but sobered up— still, they feel different. Strange. Electrified. There is, across campus, the sense that something is happening.

And something, surely, is. Even we can feel it. As students pour out into the streets, Johnny now among them, there is that feeling, that sense; for these students, tonight, right now, the world feels plastic. One of their own has gone into Main Quad and set herself on fire. This was a radical action. It demands a radical response.

Is this it? A march, a protest, nothing, in the grand scheme of things, except catharsis, a great outpouring of affect, and maybe not even the right one; no doubt as they swirl into Main Quad by the thousand, the shrewd among them are thinking ahead, thinking how they may channel this great outpouring of affect into something productive, something that will last, but for everyone else, the future is unknown and unknowable; they do not know what will happen tonight. And isn't that what's so exciting, what's so possible, about tonight, that they don't know? That the future could be anything?

Well. The thing about the present is that it's only one thing. And so as the protest grows and grows, so too does the presence of the police, who have fanned out around the crowd's edges, concentrating, particularly, in front of The Institute, emerging just a little too quickly, seeming a little too prepared, but even they don't seem particularly prepared for what happens next: something blows up in The Institute, and the glass shatters, and the alarms go off, and the students scream, and the police scream, and the students stampede, and the police fire tear gas into the charging crowd, and then it's safe to say that all hell breaks loose because what everyone hears, over the screaming, over the alarm, over the stampede, is the sound of a single gunshot, and what barely anyone sees, through the tear gas, through the bodies trampling over one another, through all hell breaking loose, is Johnny motherfucking Soufflé, hitting the ground.

Serious Business

Outside, behind a leadsmudged sky, some stars sit in the jet, burning.

Something's in the air. A thick fog's come in from the hills, and who should it be but that friendly classroom acquaintance of ours, the Real, just rolling through: over the quad, past the library, and up the Row, it's only a matter of time before he's here, coming up the patio steps, looking a little too eager. Give him a wave, a smile, a turn of the head that says you've got something else going on, you're here with friends, after all—ah: you kept staring. And now he's coming over. What else can you do but look as busy as possible and hope he'll just hang around, doing his thing, waiting for an opening. It's suffocating, isn't it? That feeling. Something heavy. Something big. Something.

But over here, one house over, there's refuge for the oblivious and the unwilling. True to their name, the Degenerates have spent the past hour withering away, bit by bit; unsure whether the vaguely cosmic boredom they feel is the heel of some great boot pressing them down, or its steel toe prodding their ribs—and ignoring it either way—they can be found, tonight, like most others, lounged across three well-fumigated, two-seater couches, arranged in an unfortunate, if familiar, L.

It's bad, this L. On some level, all parties present are privy to its faults, though with it being there before they came, and it being there since, they've rationalized their inaction as a humble acceptance of their lot, choosing to let the feng shui fester, a spiritual blunder whose physical manifest—a cornered trash can, trash spilling out like the foam of an ambitious pour—has really started to smell. So yes, everyone knows it's bad news, this L: everyone, at one point or another, having carried the weight of that most cruel and unusual burden placed upon the topmost couch dweller, presently the oldest and least senior member of the crew: a wiry, womb-obsessed film major who's grumbling indistinctly as he ferries a half-smoked spliff between couches. Excepting the obvious, a great number of solutions have been proposed—there are, let's remember, engineers in their midst. And presently, finding themselves at a conversational lull, they rehash these: wall-mounted conveyor belts, quadcopters, an appropriately sized Lazy Susan; the heretics among them suggest passing right, the dreamers telekinesis, and at last, the dialectic up and running, a new challenger approaches: the taming and training of a particularly resourceful brand of weasel, the stoat.

— So these stouts-

— Stoats.

— Huh?

— Stoats.   — Stoats.   — Stoats.

— Right so these stoats.

— Stouts, isn't it?

— Støäts. Depends where they're from.

— Look if you guys don't wanna explain this, then I'll-

— Oh c'mon, Chuck.

— Chucky.

— The Chuckster.

— WHAT?

The spliff has stopped in its tracks, somewhere in no man's land.

— Hey let's simmer it down Big C.

— Just playing around here. A bit of old fashioned joshin.

— A little yankin of the chain.

— Some pullin of the hair.

— Nothing but wholesome, affectionate kidding.

— Kiddin, Chuck, that's all it is.

— All it's ever been, really.

Here, one of the Degenerates unpeels from the couch and, splicing her words between the steps of what might be a kick-boxing routine, implores:

— Let's! Do! Something!

Like the cloud of smoke that preceded it, the suggestion floats, hangs, and fades into the air. She looks around. Disappointment palpable, she moves from couch dweller to couch dweller, summoning as much gravitas as she can muster. With a sweep of the hand, she intones:

— From the beginning of time, people have done things for many reasons. I believe it was god who did the first things. And then, once she had done some things, it was people who began to do things. Many things. Many great things. Yes my friends, it's safe to say a lot of things have been done. In fact,

I might even go as far as to argue that all of humanity has participated in the great, collective doing of things. But today, I look around, and do you know what I see? People doing nothing. No things. The end of humanity as we know it. Now, I propose to you, do we let this great experiment die? Or-

— Yes.   — Yes.   — Yes.   —Yes.   — Yes.

— Or, do we-

— I thought we agreed on dying?

— Definitely agreed on dying. Should we put it to a vote?

— All in favor?

— Fuck am I going to have to drag you-

A Degenerate extends a pair of feet, as if to say: yes.

— It's Carneval. Can we please. For once. Just. Do something!

And what do you know, maybe it's a special night, tonight. For, against all odds, after some more hemming and hawing, the Degenerates begin the lengthy process of extrication: like newly animated golems, they rise from their slouches and lumber about the room, searching for misplaced shoes, keys, and wallets, upending couch cushions, unplugging chargers, layering, delayering, bickering, and laughing as, with one sorrowful look back, they hit the light switch and walk into the night.

— I can't see shit.

An even thicker fog has settled in. It's empty out here, at the ends of West Campus. No one's drained the water in the lake, much to the relief of the frogs, whose chorus of fucking fills the night.

The Degenerates weave along, stopping at one of the intriguingly anachronistic gas lamps that light the path; they look into the fog ahead.

— Where is everyone?

— Dunno.

— Yo what the FUCK?

— What's up, Chucky?

— Check your email.

— On Carneval? I thought we agreed.

— Check your fucking email. They fucking . . . I can't even explain. What the fuck. What the fuck.

— What?

— They shot Johnny.

— What?   — What?   — What?   — What?   — What?

— Johnny motherfucking Soufflé. They fucking shot him. Like in Main Quad.

— Who shot him?

— The fucking cops. What the fuck. There was a protest . . . something about an explosion . . . and a video . . . hold on.

They hold on.

— What the actual fuck. Y'all have to see this.

They see it.

— Shit!   — Fuck!

— Fuck this, I'm going back to the suite.

— We're coming with.

So they retreat, past the intriguingly anachronistic gas lamps, past the chorus of frogs whose fucking fills then night, down the steps, along the path, and into the suite, where they resume their positions on the L, with the exception of one, who sits at the desk in the corner of the room, pinching emergency spliffage into a paper, hands shaking.

— Fuck me.

— Yeah.

— What the fuck.

— Johnny, man.

— Fuck.

— Yeah . . .

A Degenerate looks up from her phone.

— They sent another email.

— QuadSquad?

— Yeah. They found the note.

— What note?

— The girl's.

— Fuck me.

— Where'd they find it?

— Says it came in an email.

— From who?

— Says the address was just a bunch of letters and numbers.

— Weird.

— They're saying we need to read it. The link's here . . . looks long.

— I don't know.

— What?

— Feels weird.

— Shouldn't it?

— I guess.

— Fuck me.

— I mean she wanted it to be read. She wouldn't have posted it if she didn't.

— Yeah.

— I think we should read it.

— Yeah?

— What else are we going to do?

— Yeah okay.

— Out loud?

— Yeah.

— Should I or does one of y'all . . .

— Go for it.

— Okay. But no interruptions.

They nod. She takes a breath and exhales.

— 'I am not a good person. I've done something that has hurt a lot of people. The fact that I killed myself after doesn't change that. I will only hurt more.'

— 'It's been funny, writing this note. For a long time, I thought I'd be a writer. Not that I wrote. Outside of school, this is the only real writing I've done. And I liked it. I liked writing this note. It almost convinced me not to kill myself. But it didn't. And even if it had, I could've never been a writer.'

— 'I could've never been a writer because I don't believe in it. I don't think writing can meaningfully change the world. That is a statement about our world, not a statement about writing. I think writing used to have that power. Just not now. The powerful are simply too powerful. They have too much money, too many guns, and they are too organized. It's true: everything seems inescapable, until it isn't. I'm open to that possibility. But some smart guys once said that class struggles have always ended in one of two ways: revolution or ruin. It's clear which way we're headed.'

— 'The obstacle is whiteness. There are good white people, of course; there is no good whiteness. Its very existence is predicated on domination. You know the concept of the white race is a relatively recent historical invention. It has not always existed; god willing, it will not always exist. And yet, for as long as it does, it will involve this: wanting something you can't have, the pursuit of the infinite. Pursuing infinity predates white people. But we perfected it. No other group of people in the history of the world has pursued the infinite as nakedly as we have. To fear death is to desire infinite life. To be a capitalist is to desire infinite wealth. In its pursuit of goals like these, whiteness will consume everything in its path. It is not an exaggeration to say that it is apocalyptic. It destroys worlds. It has before, and it will again. That's why we have to destroy it.'

— 'Well, you do. I'm dead. But I've already done my part. We'll get to that. To explain it, I need to tell you a story. A story about what happens when you play in the dark.'

— 'It's a funny little thing, darkness. The dark. Whatever we say, I think we're all afraid of it. No real mystery why: it's the dark, and the thing about the dark is you can fill it with whatever you want. If you actually knew what was there, it wouldn't be the dark.'

— 'But that's the funny thing about the dark: most of the time, nothing's there. Nothing that wouldn't be there in the light, anyways. Did you know that with the exception of rape and car theft, most crime happens at pretty equal rates throughout the day? And while most rapes happen at night, most rapes happen at home, with people you know.'

— 'It's terrifying, the dark. When you're afraid of the dark, you're afraid of all the things that could be there. And that, when you get down to it, is really what the dark is: it's all the things that could be. I've made it sound scary, but the truth is if the dark's the land of the could be, then the dark is also where all the best things live—the dark's big enough for our dreams and our nightmares.'

— 'So what's the light? The light is rare. I'm not sure we've ever really seen it. I'm not sure we can see it. If the dark's the land of the could be, then the light is the land of what is. Sometimes what is is beautiful; you are in awe of what's there; it's sublime. But more often than not, what you experience in the light is horror: one of your terrors has stepped out of the dark, and now it's here, real. It is.'

— 'So it's no surprise we don't like to spend time there. At least, not in the total light. Of course, it's not like total darkness is any better. The terror of infinite possibilities matches the horror of a single one. So what do we do? We cast shadows. We create enough of the dark.'

— 'You can probably see where this is going. Most of us create too much of the dark. To stay in the light, really stay in it, consider the world as it is, not as it could be, not as it used to be, but as it is, every single day, it's too much. The reality is that unconscionable violence is happening every day. Palestine is happening every day. Michael Brown is happening every day. Last year, when they elected Trump, liberals lost their fucking minds. Because for a second, there was no dark. But it came back. It came back strong. America is still the darkest place of the earth. So it needs to end.'

— 'No point in subtext: I'm a communist. But I am not a revolutionary. I'm white; my family has a house in Aspen. I'm the rich they want to eat. Or would've been, anyways.'

— 'I guess what I am is a terrorist. I imagine that's what the media will call me.'

— 'I did a bad thing. I've done plenty of bad things. I was racist, for a while. Was confused about gender. I hurt people. Said things I shouldn't have. Did things I shouldn't have. When you're a teenager, it's easy to pretend like these things don't matter. But they do. It all matters.'

— 'It started because I was hurting. This excuses nothing. But it does explain something. I wanted to die. Since hitting puberty, I have spent the vast majority of my life suicidal. There is nothing romantic about this. It's just a fact. A reality of my life. A list of diagnoses might explain it. Bipolar. Gender dysphoria. OCD. Or it might not. But that's how it all started. I wanted to die.'

— 'I wanted to die, so I lived online. I lurked. I watched. I was a passive observer, until I wasn't. It started my freshman year of high school, in world geography. My friend had his laptop open. On his bookmarks bar, I saw four green leafs. The text read-' I guess it's . . . slash b slash?

— Just pronounced b, I think.

— Right. 'The text read /b/. I asked my friend what it was. He looked at me for a few seconds, then smirked. "Yeah, you're fucked up enough," he said, "but I can't show you here." I assumed it was porn. It was, and it wasn't. You've probably heard of 4chan. If you haven't, it's famous primarily for its two main exports: memes and Nazis.'

— 'You would think, me being Jewish, that as soon as I encountered this fact, which was more or less immediately, I would have never returned. The Nazi is my existential enemy. It is foundational to their belief system that someone like me—Jewish, disabled, transgender—should not exist. It's true, I wasn't trans then, nor did I see myself as disabled. But I knew I was Jewish. And if encountering the rest of the bigotry, hatred, and evil rampant on that site wasn't enough to dissuade me, then, at the very least, you would think encountering routine calls for my own extermination would be enough to push me away; it wasn't. This is a testament to my personal weakness and, I think, to the allure of whiteness.'

— 'I read once that white Jews experience a sort of double vision: looking at white goys, the white Jew feels that they are not white; looking at people of color, the white Jew feels that they are very white indeed. I know white Jews that want to be white. I know white Jews that don't want to be white. I have been both. Both are prone to upsetting behavior. I imagine that what I'm about to say is going to upset all manner of Jew, certainly my family. But what are they going to do to me?'

— 'Every white person should feel compelled to fight against white supremacy, but the white Jew should feel this acutely, for any one of six million reasons. It's a classic conundrum: our historical and lived experience of oppression should dissuade us from becoming oppressors, so how can we who have suffered so much extend the same? How can Israel exist? The reality of our world is that no amount of historical or lived experience fully accounts for the decisions we make. The fact that Israel is ruled by a regime of whiteness—that instead of a reparation for the Holocaust, we received a continuation of the very logic that inspired it—is testament to that. The things done in our name disgust me, and they should disgust you.'

— 'Of course, that's what I think now. But it's not what I thought then. Like I said, I'm not a good person. I didn't become a Nazi, but I put up with them.'

— '4chan made me feel alive. That's the honest truth. It made me feel alive in a time when I felt very dead. It was exciting. I felt like I was a part of something.'

— 'And it was entertaining. Feeling alive and being entertained are not good reasons to do something. But I'm not writing this because I want you to forgive me. I'm writing this because I want you to understand. Most people are not fascists. Nor are they revolutionaries. Most people are passive. They accept the violence that is done against them; they accept the violence that they do to others. Whether they conceive of it on these terms is irrelevant. What matters is they do it.'

— 'You often hear that there is no ethical consumption under capitalism. Capitalism is itself so inherently unethical, so the thinking goes, that there is no ethical way to consume inside it. I would go further: for as long as we participate in the capitalist world-system—which is to say, for as long as we do not dedicate our lives to fighting it—we are, to varying degrees, complicit in the violence it depends on.'

— 'You may think this unfair. Isn't it enough to survive?

To live a good life? To make a difference where we can? Is it really the case that we need to become communist revolutionaries to be good people? It may be true that it is impossible to live a purely ethical life under capitalism, but, you might think, isn't the very crux of human experience the ongoing negotiation between real and ideal, light and dark, that gray, shadowy space of imperfection in which we all live and die? And further, you might think, who the fuck are you to lecture us on living an ethical life under capitalism? You're rich; you're white; you killed yourself.'

— 'Those would all be fair points: it is, I am, and I did. But I think you know that I'm right. If you aren't committing your life to the struggle, what are you doing? Communism is the horizon of all politics. You can call it utopia, if that makes you more comfortable. But it's communism: a stateless, classless society. An ideal. One that will perhaps never be reached. And yet. To orient your politics around anything else is to accept exploitation as a fundamental necessity of social organization. That's not realism; that's cowardice.'

— 'Or maybe you're right. Maybe this is all bullshit. The product of mental illness, delusion, and guilt. Could be. That's for you to decide.'

— 'It started with 4chan. I would go there between League of Legends queues. Then more. And more. And more.'

— 'With the exception of rarely seen moderators and widely despised trip-' oh, I don't . . . she uses a slur here. I'll just . . . 'there aren't really accounts on 4chan, no profiles, no indication that you are a unique individual. You are simply anon. And because you are simply anon, you are afforded a certain

kind of freedom: the freedom to be someone else. Or, put another way, the freedom not to be yourself.'

— 'This is the freedom of fiction. And that's what /b/
is, really: fiction. On the top of the site, there is a disclaimer:
"The stories and information posted here are artistic works of
fiction and falsehood. Only a fool would take anything posted
here as fact." I guess I was a fool.'

— 'Should we care that a Nazi is hurting? That's one question 4chan poses. Alongside its mirth, there is its pain. Some
of it is the disappointment of entitlement: men disappointed
by the promise of patriarchy; white people disappointed by
the promise of white supremacy; etc. But some of it isn't. Some
of it is the pain of being a capitalist subject; some of it is the
pain of being a subject at all.'

— 'I liked the pain. It made me feel less alone. I didn't
believe everything I read, but I believed enough. We all have
our delusions. If you don't do anything with them, what does
it matter?'

— 'Unfortunately, it was on 4chan that I learned you could
do things on the internet besides consume. Sometimes you
would go offsite. And that's how it started: a raid.'

— 'A raid is just collective action online. Sometimes they
have a point; sometimes they don't. Calling for a raid often
backfires: "/b/ is not your personal army," as they say. But
sometimes things work out. In this case, it was quickly discovered that one of the targets was a fairly active user on a white
supremacist forum, one that was poorly moderated, and even
more poorly constructed, so within a few minutes, there were
dozens of new accounts posting all manner of distressing im-

age, until the moderators locked the site, and then everyone downloaded a program known as Low Orbit Ion Cannon and brought the site down. Justice was served.'

— 'This is a fairly heartwarming tale of internet fuckery, except what happened next was that someone linked a sex worker's stream in the IRC chat, and then everyone flooded in, dropping the usual trollish requests—a sharpie in the pooper, a shoe on her head—which at first the sex worker took in stride, riffing with the "virgins" and "basement dwellers," until the virgins and basement dwellers got bored, and then they started filling the chat with rape and death threats, a name, and then an address.'

— 'That's where the raid ended for me. It's where my journey should've ended entirely. But it didn't. And neither did the raid. They kept going, finding new websites to take down, Low Orbit Ion Cannon firing endlessly into the night.'

— 'I didn't go back to 4chan for a few days after that. When I did, I told myself I wouldn't go on any more raids. And I didn't, really. I kept lurking. But something had changed. I had arrived. I just needed somewhere to go.'

— 'About a month later, I found it. It was late; I was looking at a thread started by a Swedish teenager. I assumed they were a teenager. They didn't say. Their friend had died by suicide, and they blamed us. Too much time on 4chan, too much time on the "dark web." You can guess how people reacted. Someone broke out the "an hero" copypasta. Several people told the friend to kill themselves. Someone asked to see their tits. I don't know if they were a woman, but clearly they hadn't spent much time on the site. That or it was fake.

Impossible to tell.'

— 'I had seen the dark web mentioned in a few threads here and there. The Silk Road had just come online, so I knew of it mainly as a place you could buy drugs. I've always thought drugs are worthless, so I had no real interest in it, but something about that thread caught my attention. It was a meme some anon had posted, one of those iceberg ones. I don't remember what they said in the post, just that it was perfectly punctuated. Professionally so. It was unsettling. Felt out of place. But clearly they belonged; here was this meme: 4chan at the top, then, beneath the water, Tor and Anonymous, the Silk Road and Hidden Wiki, Lolita City, and, finally, at the bottom, KtZ.'

— 'I think the meme was ironic. There were other things in the iceberg that I don't remember, references to technology that didn't exist, obviously satirical government programs, and so on. No one explained, or even commented on, the meme. The thread ended a few posts later.'

— 'Depending on how you look at it, the thread came at a good or a bad time: I was pretty much burnt out on 4chan. The initial mixture of shock and excitement had worn off. Most of the memes were getting stale. If it hadn't been for the green texts, I would have already left. But I loved those little stories. Most were shitposts, but some felt like authentic slices of life, the rare bits of humanity that even 4chan couldn't digest.'

— 'Still, I was tired. But when I saw that meme, something opened up. Suddenly life felt like it was full of paths. Places to go. Things to see. I had something to do. A project.

Any thread that looked like it might have had more information, I read. This meant looking in places I didn't often want to go, but I had gotten good at dissociated scrolling. Porn threads didn't bother me. Rule 34 threads didn't bother me. Even gore. It goes without saying that certain images have stayed with me. A penis split in half with a cleaver. A man fucking a snake. A forehead bullet hole. But there was so much more that I've forgotten. Now it seems unthinkable. Then it felt basically normal. What you'd expect.'

— 'I looked offsite, too. There wasn't nearly as much information as there is now, but there was some. I read up on Tor and Anonymous. I learned more about the Silk Road. I knew enough not to google Lolita City. I couldn't find anything about KtZ.'

— 'Looking back, I guess it was just curiosity. There was something alluring about it all. The fact that it was hidden and unknown. Of course, if all you're doing is looking, there's very little you can find on the dark web that you can't find anywhere else. You don't even need to go to 4chan. You can watch people die on Facebook. You can find child porn on Feed. There are Nazis recruiting on Twitter. It's harder to find, and it gets taken down, but it's there.'

— 'Conversely, like the rest of the internet, the dark web is mostly just full of people who want your money: I'm sure if you looked hard enough, you might find a way to actually hire a hitman, but for the most part, you'll only find scams. That's most of what it is: scams, hoaxes, bullshit.'

— 'At least using Tor you have some privacy. But even then, I wouldn't count on it: my general rule of thumb is that anything you do on a computer can be traced. All technology can be broken. Everything has vulnerabilities. Nothing is safe. Not really. Ultimately, privacy is a political problem, not a technological one.'

— 'We know all this now, but in 2011, to those of us who didn't know very much, things looked a little different. We didn't know about PRISM; a fruit vendor in Tunisia had set himself on fire and Anonymous rallied behind him, doing politics from the comfort of their rooms. It was an exciting time to be online.'

— 'I read for about two weeks, and then I did two things: I downloaded Tor, and I started hanging out in Anonymous IRC chats. It didn't take long for me to get stuck. If there was a dark web search engine then, I didn't know how to use it; finding something on the dark web meant having a link to the onion site on hand. I was planning on using Hidden Wiki for this, but I soon discovered that Hidden Wiki was down.'

— 'I learned not to be surprised by stuff like this. Sites on the dark web were always going down, for any number of reasons. There was some talk in the IRC chat about FBI raids, blowback from when Anonymous had DDoS'd some credit card companies. They were withholding payments to WikiLeaks. You can look up the rest.'

— 'I don't think the FBI was going after Hidden Wiki, but for whatever reason, maybe collateral damage, it was down. I'm sure I could've found another collection of onion sites, but I had the IRC chats, and for those months, I was satisfied spending my time in #darkweb. OPSEC there was generally poor; it was meant to be an informational space, a place for anons to ask questions.'

— 'I primarily lurked. Onion sites were passed around. I would wait for someone else to vet them before looking. It was mostly discussion of markets. There was some talk of cryptocurrencies, a relatively new phenomenon at the time. I often think about how in another world, had things turned out a little differently, I would've been the teenager who bought some drugs, kept some Bitcoin, and was set a few years later. But that's how you go insane. Thinking about what could've been.'

— 'The chat had a few admins. Most were fine, but there was one who made me uneasy. Their handle was just the letters gm, close to my initials. Or what they were then. They were confrontational, fairly paranoid, and prone to privately messaging suspicious members of the chat; a subsequent ban was not uncommon. I tread carefully, saying very little.'

— 'My private chat came a few days after joining.' . . . and then it's like a chat . . . I guess I'll just read . . .

— 'gm: what's your deal?'

— 'alex: what do you mean?'

— 'gm: you never say anything. never share links.'

— 'gm: are you a fed?'

— 'alex: would i tell you if i was?'

— 'gm: not a good response'

— 'alex: i'm just looking around'

— 'gm: also not a good response. strike 2'

— 'alex: i want to know more about KtZ'

— 'There was a long pause before their next response.'

— 'gm: how does a new-' . . . another slur here . . . 'like you know about KtZ'

— 'alex: 4chan'

— 'gm: of course'

— 'gm: last i heard KtZ is dying'

— 'alex: what do you mean?'

— 'Another pause.'

— 'gm: fucking hell'

— 'gm: no way you're a fed because no way a fed would be this stupid'

— 'gm: please tell me alex isn't your actual name'

— 'alex: it's not'

— 'gm: good'

— 'gm: you're on thin ice'

— 'The chat ended there. #darkweb had died down for the night. I hung around in the general chat and mindlessly read a few threads. Then I went to sleep.'

— 'A few months passed without any real incident. I went to school. I learned more. I watched as Anonymous took down the Playstation Network, and the gamers turned on them. Hidden Wiki was still down, but I found plenty. Still, nothing about KtZ.'

— 'Then, one night, I got another message. At this point, fearing a ban, I had started to contribute more to the chat. Not very much, but enough to keep me afloat. Most people kept the same handle, so it was easy enough to track who was who. There was a particularly vicious flamewar unfolding that night. LulzSec had gone to war with the Arizona border patrol. The chat was divided. I was staying out of it, obviously.'

— 'So it was a surprise when one of the regulars in the chat messaged me.'

— 'fedagent: are you the one looking for KtZ?'

— 'Since my conversation with gm, I hadn't mentioned anything about KtZ in the chat. They had been talking. I felt sick.'

— 'alex: i was'

— 'fedagent: you gave up?'

— 'alex: sort of'

— 'fedagent: i found this'

— 'He sent a link to an onion site. I didn't click it.'

— 'alex: how do i know that's not CP'

— 'fedagent: you just have to trust me'

— 'fedagent: but you can'

— 'fedagent: i am a federal agent, after all'

— 'I went to the site. It was a picture of a naked woman against a black background. She was blindfolded. It was impossible to tell what she was feeling. She looked young.'

— 'alex: what is this'

— 'fedagent: it's nice, right?'

— 'alex: what is it'

— 'fedagent: it's nice'

— 'I didn't respond. Then, a minute or two later,'

— 'fedagent: it's part of KtZ'

— 'alex: what is KtZ?'

— 'fedagent: progress'

— 'fedagent: civilization'

— 'fedagent: the peak'

— 'fedagent: you'll see'

— 'I stared at the screen. They didn't say anything else, and neither did I. Some time passed; I became contemplative. It occurred to me in that moment how still everything was: the only things moving in my room were the fans, one on the ceiling, a pair in my computer, which, either too weak or too dirty, did not seem to be able to keep up with the heat my computer generated, loudly exhausting themselves, as they did every night, while I sat at my computer, alone, afraid, my brain the opposite of still, not quite the picture of depression one often encounters, one of absence, vacancy, anhedonia, as if the depressed person's brain were simply empty and not, as in my case, full, active, flooded with thoughts every second of every day: kill yourself. I felt small in that stillness, smaller than I had felt in a long time. I felt anonymous. Insofar as anyone was paying attention to my life, they were paying attention to a lie. It's truly astonishing the depths of psychic pain you can hide behind some good grades and a bad haircut.'

— 'I have never been honest with anyone about how much I've thought about killing myself. It's easier here because I've already done it. Just believe me that this has nothing to do with pity. I only want to be understood. What I'm about to say I assign no valence; it's just the truth: my experience of growing up suicidal was the single most important experience in my life. It is also what I consider my most authentic experience, the very core of who I am. And no one knows. The version of myself they know is simply a veil. This is, of course, true for everyone. We all have a private psychic world that we can only communicate in varying degrees of abstraction. I won't pretend my psychic world is any more real or vivid or interesting than anyone else's; in fact, I would wager that in some sense, it's significantly more abstract. This is what being wealthy and white enables you to do: to live abstractly, to live in the darkness. I think it's fair to say that I know very little about the real world. I have been insulated from it my whole life, by wealth, by whiteness, by mental illness. What could I possibly know about the zeitgeist? This is all just text to me. Something on a page. Shit on a screen. My life is the product of a genuinely unthinkable amount of real human suffering, and that's what's significant to me about KtZ, something I knew as little about, sitting in that chair, listening to those fans, as you do now. But do you see why I am telling you all of this? What the point is? They were right about KtZ. It is progress. It is civilization. I don't know that I need to say more. You don't need these things explained to you, and certainly not by me. You just need to know about KtZ. So fine. Take a breath. We'll get there.'

The Degenerate reading stops to take a breath. A few of her compatriots have drifted off, not quite unfocused, not quite asleep. Noises from the darkness fill the empty space. It's late. It's night.

— 'I stared at the screen,' she begins again, — 'and I kept staring. The next three weeks were annoying. A new group of trolls called 3E appeared; they were making the chats basically unusable. There was nothing artful about their trolling. It was just spam. Three weeks of slurs and spam.'

— 'I almost left for good. Hidden Wiki was still down. No one was volunteering information about KtZ, and I didn't dare ask; the truth is I didn't really care anymore. Everything was shit and getting worse. You can imagine.'

The Degenerate stops again.

— There's a section break.

— A what?

— Like a two. Well, a two in Roman numerals.

— Fuck.

— I'll just . . . 'One night, after a game of League, I logged on; most everyone was offline, except for two anons.'

— 'avunc: how'd they do it?

— 'nepo: no one knows. some zero day'

— 'nepo: they got access and wiped everything out'

— 'nepo: used KtZ lmao'

— 'nepo: the rest is history'

— 'avunc: lmfao. i'm sure they loved that'

— 'nepo: ofc'

— 'So it was something you could use. I immediately assumed it was malware of some kind. There was enough of that out there; the more infosec-inclined anons would chat about it sometimes, but I had never really looked into it. I went to one of the forums they linked once. Didn't understand most of what was happening. Didn't want to download the wrong thing.'

— 'alex: what does KtZ do?'

— 'They didn't respond. An hour later, someone came in the chat and started it up again. They had found a new market. I played more League. When I went to bed, I could see it flicker on the inside of my eyes.'

— 'A few days passed; 3E finally burnt out on their trolling campaign. Or they found somewhere new to go. Either way, they were gone.'

— 'Then life got kind of interesting. Hidden Wiki came back online, and #darkweb splintered. There was some sort of dispute between gm and one of the other admins. Whatever it was, it didn't happen in a public channel. This was a key feature of life in the IRC chats. There were always backchannels, new groups, new factions, the strong sensation that things were happening somewhere you couldn't see. I can't imagine what it would've been like if you really wanted to be on the inside. The doubt and paranoia. The feeling that you were being left out of something. At any rate, I went with gm and a few of the other chat members. I figured that was my best chance.'

— 'There was a meme that used to float around 4chan, maybe it still does: born too late to explore the earth, born too early to explore the galaxy. Something like that. A colonist's dream cloaked in the language of childhood wonder. It's all just infinity, of course: the pursuit of novelty, the fetish of progress. Behind it all is a very simple logic. Accumulation. That's all it is. Accumulate wealth. Accumulate land. Accumulate experiences. Get more. Be more.'

— 'The problem has never been clearer: a finite people living on a finite earth, both stretched to infinity by the demands of capital. It breaks us, like it breaks the earth, like it's supposed to break itself. Maybe one day it will. For your sake, I hope so.'

— 'Probably this is all a little too obvious. By now, it should be clear that I am not speaking to you from a position of political enlightenment or moral authority. If I were a good person, I would be out doing the work, not dead. What I am, what I was, is sick. When you look closely enough, it's sort of impossible to divorce my worldview from my experience of mental illness: the exaggerated feelings of guilt, the worthlessness, the grandiosity, the simultaneous belief that everything can change and nothing can. I see its shadow everywhere. A state to end all states. A class to end all classes. It's all some kind of suicide, really. Not that that makes it any less right. I'm not a communist because of guilt or grandiosity or some twisted understanding of suicidality; I'm a communist because people are suffering. Real people. You're probably one of them. People are suffering, and they don't need to be. Only history tells us that we need to exploit one another to survive.'

— 'I don't know why I'm explaining this. I know that you know that I know that I am a piece of shit in exactly the same way that many Harvard and Stanford and certainly University students-'

— Uh oh.

— Shh.

— 'that many Harvard and Stanford and certainly University students are pieces of shit: unremarkably. But at least I'm not trying to sell you anything. I just put this online, for free. And then I set myself on fire. No one is getting anything out of this.'

— 'KtZ. I'd find it soon. But not before a few things happened. The first was, surprisingly, nice. Maybe the only good thing to come out of all this. Deep in the archives of one of those market forums, I found a link to an unpublished novel. The title was To The Thief. The PDF was encrypted. The post was two words long: "hurry up."'

— 'It didn't really bother me that I couldn't read the novel. It felt right. The novel being there. An unreadable and artistic work of fiction and falsehood. It was a heartening moment.'

— 'What happened next was not. I remember exactly what I was doing. I was eating. It must've been sometime after Tuesday because I was eating leftover macarrones, Tuesday's meal. I had heaped a pile of them on a plate, covered it with cheddar jack and parmesan, and nuked it in the microwave; I ate it in my room, with a glass of milk.'

— 'Since downloading that PDF, I had had the strong suspicion that something was going on. Sites were going down faster than usual. It was getting harder to find anything. A few of the chat regulars had disappeared. There were references to conversations I wasn't a part of, decisions that had been made. But what else was I going to do? I crawled through the fog. I felt I was close. And I was.'

— 'The private message came from a handle I didn't recognize. The first thing they sent was an onion link. The second was a name: hman, the handle of one of the missing chat regulars. The link took me to a grainy video. All you could really see was a chair sitting in a concrete room. A man in the chair. His bloody face. His hands tied behind his back. Nothing moved for a few seconds. Then there was a gunshot. I closed out of the tab before I could see anything else; I went back to the chat. There was a new link. I didn't want to see what was there. I really shouldn't have. But I did. It took me to a picture. It was an image from Google Maps. My house, seen from the street. On the second floor, through those windows, you could see my younger brother, working at his desk. Book open. Head down. Shades up. Totally oblivious.'

— 'I got up and stood outside his room. The strip of space beneath his door was dark. He was asleep. I went back to my room.'

— 'The chat was in a frenzy. I was not the only one who had received the video. But no one said anything about being sent a picture of their house. I watched the chat go. Some thought the video was fake. Others thought it was real. I didn't know what to think. It all suddenly felt so absurd. 4chan. The chat. This journey. KtZ. All of it. A few years later, about a year ago, I felt something like that again, coming down from my first psychosis. It's not so surprising. Everything feels absurd in the light. Without darkness, without narrative, there can be no explanation, no meaning, no motion. No connection between things. Everything simply is. It just is.'

— 'You know, it's funny. For you, reading this now, without me saying it, it would be impossible to tell that I just experienced another one of those moments. Just now. As I was writing. I went out for a cigarette. And as I sat there, staring over Lake Bog, listening to all those fucking frogs, I really did feel it: the absurdity of my plan. Unleashing KtZ on the world, to say nothing of the rest: to go into Main Quad, to set myself on fire. As if that would do anything except traumatize whoever found me. Would you believe that I almost deleted all of this? That I almost made it to the hospital?'

— 'Exterminate. That was the word that accompanied KtZ, when I finally found it. There was a single-word readme, and that was what it said: exterminate. I can't imagine anything more fitting.'

— 'I was basically there. I couldn't sleep. A few hours later, at 3 or 4 in the morning, the final message came. Someone else I didn't recognize' . . . I think it's Russian.

— What is?

— The name.

— Let me see.

She hands them the phone.

They look.

They hand the phone back.

— Pronounced 'arlekin.'

— Got it.

— 'arlekin: hello'

— 'alex: hello'

— 'arlekin: do you want to meet KtZ?'

— 'alex: it's a person?'

— 'arlekin: no'

— 'arlekin: but it is something you meet'

— 'alex: yes'

— 'alex: i want to meet it, i mean'

— 'arlekin: i heard you found my novel'

— 'alex: what'

— 'arlekin: my novel. to the thief.'

— 'arlekin: they said you found it'

— 'alex: who did'

— 'arlekin: you're going to like KtZ i think'

— 'arlekin: it will be good for your brain'

— 'arlekin: it was for mine'

— 'arlekin: haha' . . . another section break.

— Fuck.

— 'I stared. And then I asked for the link. They sent it.'

— 'It's just a dataset. That's all it is. A couple datasets. Text. Images. Videos. There's terabytes and terabytes. Any document of barbarity you can think of, KtZ has it. Probably hundreds of it. Snuff. CP. Gore. It's all there, diligently labeled, ready to be learned from. I don't know if anyone had tried using it as a training set before, or if it was just a hypothetical, a thought experiment: what would happen if you trained a machine learning model on the very worst humanity has to offer? I guess you'll see.'

— 'arlekin explained all of this. For years, they had just been a troll, content to raise a bit of hell online. And then, much like me, they had become enamored with the possibility of something deep, dark, and hidden. They discovered a reference to KtZ in some forum. They pursued it. They found it. It did something to their brain. They had spent years with it, watching it grow and grow and grow.'

— 'alex: someone said KtZ was dying'

— 'arlekin: it's too big'

— 'alex: too big?'

— 'arlekin: impossible to download without giving yourself away'

— 'arlekin: it'd be a suicide mission'

— 'arlekin: it's being watched'

— 'alex: so what does it do'

— 'arlekin: it exists'

— 'arlekin: sometimes it grows'

— 'I didn't know what to say. They didn't either. The

conversation ended. I looked at the readme. I saved the onion site. I closed the page. And then that was it. I couldn't download it. I couldn't even look at it.'

– 'It was done. I went back to my life. Eventually, I stopped wanting to kill myself for long enough that the next time it happened, I was surprised. Or maybe just disappointed.'

— 'I wish that I could tell you that I did what I did for noble reasons. If I did, it wouldn't necessarily be a lie. There are a lot of ways to kill yourself. Very few of them involve deliberate sabotage. But that wasn't really why I killed myself. I killed myself because I was in pain and my life was not worth the suffering it takes to sustain it. Not mine and not others'.'

— 'At some point in college, I felt guilty about all the time I had spent on the internet. And I wanted some of my own money to spend. So I got a job content moderating. I was a digital janitor, underpaid, exploited, and somewhat fulfilled. I looked at murders and people fucking kids, and I flagged everything. I'm sure some of the videos I've seen, the images I've seen, the things I've read, I'm sure it's all there. Part of KtZ. I was doing redundant work. But I wasn't going to complain. I was getting paid the same.'

— 'As for what I did, it was fairly straightforward. I made friends with one of the disgruntled engineers. I listened to him complain about his life. I reminded him that no matter how much he was being paid, he, too, was a worker being exploited. I stoked the flames. And then I explained my plan. I reassured him that I would take the fall. I found KtZ again. It was no longer 2011. Things were easier now. We figured out a way to download it. And then we poisoned the well. If you can read this faster than they can, you may catch a glimpse of it. Some people will. Of that much I'm sure. But word travels fast. So now Feed has a choice. Let it flow or shut it all down.'

— It's down now.

— Feed?

— Yeah.

— Fuck.

— Down for me too.

— There's a bit more. In the note.

— Go for it.

— 'I found the woman. The blindfolded one. It was a few weeks after I had found KtZ. I was still on 4chan. She was doing a thread. She had just turned eighteen. But it was her. She had the same birthmark, creeping up her neck. I read through the thread. Saw the usual requests. Saw her deliver. Then, for the first time, I posted. The link to KtZ. She didn't respond. No one else did either. I'm sure everyone thought it was spam. A few days later, I redownloaded Tor and put in the link, just to see. It was down.'

— 'But she was real. I know that now. KtZ is the light. Nothing more, nothing less. It has no narrative. It doesn't need it. arlekin said it was all real. Real data. Real horror. And it is. It is.'

— …

— …   — …   — …

— …   — …

— It's over.

Almost morning now: outside, the jet fades; inside, something heavy. The Degenerates are silent.

And fuck if we aren't too. She just doesn't . . . we told her! We told her it wouldn't hold. Fuck. And now everything's falling apart.

Sunday

Nothing is more difficult than writing an autobiography.

— ALEXANDRA KOLLONTAI

Morning

The first time I talked to God I was at lunch. Usually during lunch I like to go outside because lunch is right before recess and since Mom always packs me lunch I can go straight to the playground. But it was raining and they don't let us outside when it rains which meant I had to go to the cafeteria. Sometimes when you're late to lunch there aren't any seats next to anyone you know so you have to sit with people you've never met before which is what happened that day because I went to the bathroom at the end of class and when I got back the class was empty and Ms. Pepper said everyone was already at lunch. So I ended up sitting with some of the sixth graders which was fine with me because they don't talk to you if you don't talk to them and I'm okay eating alone.

I didn't have that much to think about so I listened to the sixth graders as they talked. They were talking about a girl named Isabel and her bra. I didn't know what that was and I wasn't going to ask but then God said *32B*. I thought God was supposed to talk in words so I asked what that meant and God said *tell them, my son, 32B.*

So I said 32B. The sixth graders looked at me funny and

then the biggest one said that I probably didn't even know what a bra was. I told them I didn't but it was 32B and they all laughed and one of them asked how I could know how big Isabel's bra was if I didn't know what a bra was. I didn't want to say God told me so I didn't say anything and they all started laughing so loud that Ms. Pepper came over and told me it was time to go back to the classroom.

I was bored in class so I asked God questions. Sometimes I have a hard time paying attention in class. Ms. Pepper says that if I spend all my time staring into space I'll have to repeat the first grade but I don't think it'd be that bad. Billy Bean-Couscous is repeating the first grade and he says it's more fun the second time around.

On the way home I asked my babysitter Allison about bras. She said I shouldn't do that. I said I was sorry and she said it was okay so I just looked out the window at the other cars.

At dinner I told my parents I talked to God. Mom looked at Dad who looked at Mom and then they both looked at me and I didn't know which of them to look at so I just looked between them. They asked me what God said and I told them 32B and they asked what that meant so I told them what happened at lunch. Then I asked Dad what a bra was and he told me to ask Mom who looked at Dad and called him Eliot which meant he shouldn't do that. Mom said that I didn't need to worry about bras right now because I was just a boy. I was going to ask why I didn't need to worry but then they asked me what God sounded like and that stumped me for a while because God didn't really sound like anything I had ever heard before. I said that I thought it sounded like how the ocean would sound if it could talk but that didn't seem to help them much so I told them that I'd talk to God later and try and figure it out. Then I smiled and they smiled and no one said anything for a while so I finished my plate and asked if I could leave the table.

I kept thinking about it but I couldn't figure it out so I left God alone and went to bed. I was trying to fall asleep but every time I try and fall asleep I stay up because I start thinking about falling asleep and once I start thinking about falling asleep I can never do it. Sometimes if it's really late I'll turn off the night-light. Usually I sleep with my night-light on because I don't like it when I can't see and it's totally dark because when I can't see and it's totally dark I start to think about that day at the Exploratorium and when I start to think about that day at the Exploratorium I start to think about that dark maze that I went into without Mom and Dad and I remember the dark and the walls and feeling like someone was blowing a balloon up in my stomach because I started to think I would never get out ever and then I was screaming screaming screaming until they turned on all the lights and someone had to drag me out. And whenever I start to think about that my stomach starts to feel the balloon and I have to breathe until it all goes away. That's why I don't like to be in the dark.

But that night I had tried almost everything and it was pretty late so I turned off the light. Then God said *watch this* and in my head I could see my whole room like it was daytime. I could see all my books and my toys and my table and then I started to see the entire house. I saw my closet and my bathroom and the living room and the kitchen and I could see Mom asleep and Dad in his office. Then everything went back to normal.

I asked God if I could see other countries and also the desert and also the bottom of the ocean where the giant squids live. I like giant squids. But I've only seen pictures of them when they're dead and on the beach. I couldn't see any giant squids so I thought that maybe God was like Google and could only take one question at a time. I was tired so I said thank you and went to sleep.

The next day was Saturday which meant there was no school and when there's no school I can sleep for as long as I want. But I wanted to wake up early so I could talk with God. It turns out God knows everything. All the capitals and all the rivers and even all the different kinds of mamba. There's four which is something most people don't know. They think it's just green and black.

The next morning I let God sleep because Sunday mornings are Family Breakfast and I didn't know if God was invited. For Family Breakfast Mom likes to cook pancakes with chocolate and raspberries and blueberries. She also puts bananas in Dad's pancakes but I don't like the smell.

We talked about pancakes for a bit and then Mom asked how talking to God was going. I said it was good and that God knew a lot and also that God showed me my room. Mom asked what that meant so I told them. That's when Mom looked at Dad but Dad just stared at his pancakes. Mom was about to say something but then I think Dad got an idea because he stood up and left the table which meant Family Breakfast was over.

I was excited when Dad told me he wanted me to talk to God. He's been working on God for a long time. He said all they would have to do to install God was touch my ear and he asked if I was okay with that. I said yes so we went to his office and they touched my ear and then nothing happened until 32B.

The next day was Monday which meant show and tell. I usually don't have anything to show and I don't like to talk in front of all the other people because when I see everybody looking at me I start to feel the balloon in my stomach and then I have a hard time talking. So I only go up when Ms. Pepper asks me if I have anything because I think that's her way of telling me I have to. Usually I try to pay attention during show and tells but that day Sam Tripe was showing his frog Big G and Sam Tripe brings his frog Big G every time we do show and tell so it wasn't that interesting.

As soon as Sam was done I heard God say *go forth and speak of me.* I asked if that meant I should raise my hand and God said *yes* so I raised my hand and said that I had something to share. When I told the class that I was talking to God everyone started to giggle. Then when I said that God could only take one question at a time but also knew everything everyone started laughing so hard that Ms. Pepper had to scream to get everyone to calm down. Ms. Pepper told me that it was very nice of me to share but then Sam stood up and said that if I was really talking to God then God could tell me how many fingers he was holding up behind his back.

Two God said so I told the class it was two and then no

one laughed because Sam brought out his hand and he was holding up two fingers. I told them that they could ask me anything so Sam asked me what the biggest city in the world was. I said that it was Tokyo but I didn't need God to tell me that one so I told him he should ask me something else. Then Louise Hen-Son stood up and said that I was just lucky and that her sister said that only crazy people heard voices in their head and then half the class started screaming *CRA-ZY! CRA-ZY! CRA-ZY!* and the other half of the class started screaming *God-Boy! God-Boy!* and I didn't know what to do so I sat on the floor. Then Ms. Pepper screamed at everyone to be quiet and took me into the hall.

The first thing she did was give me a big hug like Mom does if I'm upset. Then she told me I wasn't crazy and that she had imaginary friends when she was my age too. It looked like she was going to cry so I hugged her back and told her that I didn't think I was crazy and that I didn't care what the other kids thought because if the other kids thought I was crazy and didn't talk to me I could always just talk to God. It sounded like people were screaming in the class so I asked her if she was ready to go back inside. She nodded and I smiled and she smiled and then we both went back into the classroom.

After that some of the other kids started to call me God-Boy. A couple of them like Louise Hen-Son said they wouldn't talk to me because they thought they might catch the crazy but I didn't mind that much. I didn't talk to most of them anyways especially not Louise Hen-Son. Billy Bean-Couscous asked me if God knew whether he'd have to repeat the first grade again and God said *no* which made Billy happy because he said he didn't think first grade would be as much fun the third time around. Then Billy asked if God really knew the answer to everything and I told him that I was pretty sure God did and that made Billy even happier. Billy told me to find him the next day at recess because he had an idea that would make us both rich.

Just before school was over Ms. Pepper told me I had to stay behind because she was going to call my parents. I told her that my parents already knew about God and that I thought they wouldn't want to be called at work. She said that even though she understood what I was saying she had to do it anyways. Ms. Pepper says stuff like that a lot. As soon as she got on the phone she started to say she was sorry. I told God that Mom and Dad were probably upset that Ms. Pepper had called them during work but I didn't feel bad for Ms. Pepper because I told her and she didn't listen. That was the first time I heard God laugh. It sounded like breaking glass.

Ms. Pepper said that Mom had told her to tell me that Allison wouldn't be driving me home and that I should wait for her to come pick me up. No one was on the playground so I sat on the swings and waited for Mom's car to show up. Mom drives a Red Proja Model 3 with license plate 7CBW361. I know so as soon as I see the car I can go straight to it without her having to get out.

While I was waiting on the swings God started to play a movie in my head. At first I didn't know what was going on because all I saw was white and I thought that maybe I had accidentally been staring at the sun for too long and gone blind. Sometimes I like to look at the sun for a second or two before it starts to hurt even though I know I'm not supposed to. But then I realized I was just seeing lambs. Then one of the lambs started to bleed and every lamb the blood touched started to bleed until all the lambs were bleeding so much they were almost swimming in it. I asked God to turn it off because Mom and Dad don't like me watching bloody movies but it kept going. Then I heard Mom's voice and the movie ended so I went to the car.

Mom didn't say anything when I got in the car which made me scared. The whole car ride home no one said anything except for the people on the radio. Mom's station doesn't play any music and all the people on it always talk like they're trying not to get caught talking in the library.

When we got home I sat in the living room while Mom cooked dinner. Then we waited for Dad. When Dad got home me and Mom and Dad had a Talk. It went like this.

First Mom tells Dad that he has to take me to see Dr. T.

I tell Mom and Dad that I don't like going to see Dr. T.

Mom tells me that I have to see Dr. T.

Mom tells Dad that she can't drive me there so Dad will have to drive me.

Dad tells Mom that he has meetings all day and can't leave work on Wednesday.

Mom tells Dad that she can't drive me there so he is going to drive me.

I ask Mom and Dad why I have to go to see Dr. T.

Both Mom and Dad look at me and don't say anything and then Mom says that Ms. Pepper called and said that I told the whole class I had been talking with God.

I ask Mom and Dad what I did wrong.

Mom says that I didn't listen when they told me not to tell anyone else about God.

I say that God told me to tell everyone else about God.

Dad says that I'm going to see Dr. T.

And that was the end of the Talk.

The next day at school Billy found me at recess. He said that if we made people pay one dollar to ask God a question we could be rich. I thought about it and then I told Billy that I asked God a lot of questions and I never had to pay so I didn't think it was fair that other people had to. Billy didn't look very happy. But then he said that I was right and that it made a lot more sense if people just had to pay once at the start of the month and then that way they could ask God as many questions as they wanted. I asked God if that was fair and God said *yeah* so I told Billy it was okay. He rubbed his hands together like he was cold and then he went around the playground telling everyone that today they could ask God all the questions they wanted.

Usually nobody passes me notes during class but after recess everyone was passing me notes with questions for God. Sam Tripe wanted to know where Big G was and Liz Fish wanted to know what the moon tasted like and Max Smith wanted to know if he was going to be taller than his brother and Louise Hen-Son wanted to know all the answers to the math homework but I told her that was cheating and I wouldn't tell her which turned out to be a bad idea because then Louise Hen-Son told Ms. Pepper that I was passing notes and I got in trouble so Ms. Pepper took me out into the hallway again.

Ms. Pepper looked at me and I looked at Ms. Pepper and then before Ms. Pepper could say anything God said *summer sky*. I told God I was busy but then God said *summer sky* again so I asked what it meant. Ms. Pepper was saying something about how it wasn't fair of me to charge the other kids money to ask God questions when God finally responded and said *tell her that if she doesn't behave, everyone will see summer sky*. I told God that I didn't think Ms. Pepper would like it if I was the teacher but then God said *do it* so I did it.

I was right. Ms. Pepper didn't look very happy. She looked at me for a long time and then she asked me how I knew about summer sky. I told her that God told me to say it. She asked me how God knew about summer sky and I told her that God knew everything. Then I told her I was sorry for acting like the teacher. She said that it was okay but that it was important I didn't tell anyone else about summer sky even if God said to. I said I wouldn't and she said I had to promise and I said I promised I wouldn't. She still looked really scared so I told her I was pretty sure it was still spring and I think that helped because she finally smiled and I smiled and then I asked if we could go back into the classroom.

When we got back in the classroom Ms. Pepper said that it was quiet time so I went and got my book from my cubby. Ms. Pepper stared at her computer for the rest of the class. I think maybe she was watching a movie.

That night I couldn't sleep because Mom and Dad were arguing in their room. Mom was saying Dad shouldn't have named it God and Dad was saying that it had to be named God and Mom was saying that it really didn't and Dad was saying that it really did.

I realized that I had never asked God what name I should use. God said *God is fine* and I thought about telling Mom and Dad but I don't think they would have been happy if they knew I was listening. I asked God to play some music until they stopped fighting and then I went to bed.

The next day at school we had a sub so God and I answered a lot of questions. Usually I don't like talking to that many people but with God there it was okay. I felt pretty safe. No balloon. I told God I liked having a new friend. I didn't hear anything back but I wasn't surprised because sometimes it's hard to think of what to say so usually when that happens I just smile. I bet God smiled too.

It was a pretty good day but then I remembered that it was Wednesday and I had to go see Dr. T. I don't think Dad wanted to go see Dr. T either because when he picked me up he was making the same face he makes when he's watching the TV. I asked Dad if he was sure we had to go but he just nodded.

It took us about half an hour to get there. Dad and Dr. T work at the same company. eXe has a lot of buildings. Dad works in C but Dr. T is in H. I asked Dad if the people he worked with ever got lost and he smiled and said they were all kind of lost. I think that was Dad telling a joke. Sometimes it's hard to tell.

When we got to Dr. T's office we had to wait for fifteen minutes in the other room because the door was shut and that meant someone else was in there. Outside of Dr. T's door is a little thing that makes a lot of noise and sounds kind of like a fan. Dr. T said it was so that people didn't listen at the door. Once I asked him if that happened a lot and he said it happens more than you think which didn't make sense to me because I didn't think anyone would want to listen to Dr. T talk.

When the other people finally came out of Dr. T's office it was another family. There was a Mom and a Dad and a kid who must've been pretty old because he was taller than the Dad and the Mom and he had hair that went all the way down to his shoulders which made me jealous because Mom says I'm not old enough to choose how long my hair is. But then we heard Dr. T's voice telling us to come in so Dad and I went into his office.

Dr. T said hello to Dad and hi to me and then he told us to sit down. I was in a bad mood because I don't like seeing Dr. T because Dr. T's office is always too cold and there's nothing to look at except Dr. T and his chair and every time I see Dr. T he makes me do the same puzzles like he thinks I forget how to do them.

Dr. T smiled at me and then he said that Mom had already told him about what had happened and he asked Dad if he had anything else to add but Dad didn't so he told Dad he could wait outside until we were done. Then Dad left and Dr. T started asking me all sorts of questions about God. He asked how long I had been talking to God and when I talked to God and what God sounded like and what sorts of things God told me. I told him all about God and the whole time his head nodded up and down like it was on a spring. When I told him that God popped the balloon in my stomach he smiled and made a little note in his book.

Once he finished asking me about God he took out the puzzles and we did those for a while. The first puzzle he gave me was the one with the red and black blocks where he shows me a picture and I have to make the blocks look like the picture. Then we did a bunch of new puzzles. There was a line puzzle and a face puzzle and even a puzzle puzzle. When we finished he asked me if I wanted anything to eat but I wasn't hungry so I said no and Dr. T asked me to wait outside while he talked to Dad.

Dad didn't say anything about Dr. T on the way home. I asked him if Dr. T ever made him solve puzzles but he just shook his head which meant he didn't want to talk. We were on the highway but I couldn't look in the other cars because we were going pretty fast so I just looked at the signs. Then I saw one of the cars ahead of us start to wobble. It was a red Proja Model 3 but its license plate was 6ANM977. It was wobbling pretty bad and then it turned into the other lane and there were a lot of horns but the other cars were going too fast and a big silver car hit the red car and the red car went into the air and started doing somersaults. Then two more cars hit the big silver car. I was about to start screaming but then everything was back to normal and I realized it was one of God's movies.

Then something weird happened because we started slowing down and when I looked out the window I saw a big line of cars so I asked Dad what happened and he said it looked like there was a crash. But it was worse than a normal crash because most crashes have two cars but this one had four and one of them was upside-down. It looked like someone was playing Hot Wheels but forgot to clean up. Then something really weird happened because the car that was upside down was red and when we drove by I saw its license plate and it was 6ANM977!

I asked how God knew the cars were going to crash. God didn't say anything so I asked if God made the cars crash and God still didn't say anything which is what I do when Mom asks me if I did something and I know I'll get in trouble. Finally God said *the bourgeois parasite had it coming*. I wasn't sure what that meant so I asked Dad if he knew what a bourgeois parasite was and Dad asked how I knew what a bourgeois parasite was and I told Dad that God told me that God had caused that car crash because the bourgeois parasite had it coming. Dad seemed really surprised and he turned to look at me and then he said that he would turn God off when we got home and then out of nowhere another car hit our car and we started spinning and spinning and spinning and there was a lot of honking and yelling and I started screaming and Dad started screaming and I thought we were going to die.

We didn't die. As soon as we stopped spinning Dad got out of the car to see what had happened. I stayed in the car and when Dad got back in I asked him what happened and he said that the damage wasn't that bad but that the other car had driven off and then he said a lot of words I'm not supposed to repeat and that if he ever caught the person who did it he would make sure they were sorry.

But I knew that wasn't going to happen because I knew it was God's fault. I told God that that's not the kind of thing friends do and I wasn't going to talk to him until I got an apology. I didn't hear anything and that made me even madder because I knew that God heard me.

When we got home Mom had already made dinner so Dad and I went straight to the table. I forgot to wash my hands but so did Dad so I think it was okay. Mom asked Dad how his day was but Dad just started eating and didn't say anything. Mom looked at Dad and then at me and I told her about the accident. Dad dropped his fork and said that it was fine and that he would handle it and Mom gave him a look but Dad didn't see. I wanted to tell her that it wasn't Dad's fault because God made the other car hit us but I didn't want God to hear.

No one said anything for a while and then Mom asked how it went with Dr. T and I told her it was okay and he made me do some new puzzles and Mom said that was nice and looked at Dad but Dad just shook his head. She asked a couple more questions but I didn't want to talk anymore and neither did Dad so we all just ate without talking.

That night it was raining. I tried to read in my room but all I could hear was the rain and Mom and Dad yelling at each other. Every once in a while the thunder would go BOOM and the whole house would light up. I tried to sleep for a while but it was so loud I couldn't. I even turned off the night light but I still couldn't fall asleep and then there was a big flash and I heard something crash so I ran to the kitchen to see if something fell. But I couldn't see anything out the windows so I got a glass of milk and started to go back to my room. The light in Dad's office was on so I stopped to look in. At first I thought Dad was sleeping because he had his head on the table like Billy Bean-Couscous does when he sleeps in class. But Billy never shakes when he's sleeping.

I had never seen Dad cry. I wanted to say something but then I thought Dad might get mad if he caught me up so late so I went back to my room. And then I sat on my bed for a long time.

I just wanted Dad to be happy. And Mom too. So I told God that I was sorry I got mad and asked if there was anything God could do. Even though I didn't hear anything back God must've done something because later that night I heard Mom saying God's name. She sounded happy.

The next day I got ready to go to school but when I went into the kitchen for breakfast Mom and Dad were both sitting there and then we had another Talk.

First Mom says I don't have to go to school until next week.

I ask Mom why I don't need to go to school.

Mom says a lot happened this week.

I ask if Allison is coming over.

Mom says that Allison is busy but that Mom would take time off of work to spend time with me.

Mom never takes time off of work so I am confused.

Then Dad says that he turned off God.

I say that I thought God just made a bad decision.

Dad says God isn't supposed to make bad decisions.

I ask why not.

Dad says because I didn't build it that way.

I look at Dad.

Dad looks at me.

I say I think we should give God another chance.

Dad says no.

Mom says no.

I say okay.

And that was the end of the second Talk.

Mom and I watched a lot of TV and read together but nothing really happened until Saturday when I was sitting on my bed and God came back and showed me a video of a girl on fire. I kept telling God to turn it off but God wouldn't listen so I said that I would scream and tell Dad. God said *don't do that* and turned off the video.

Then God asked how I felt about the video. I told God I didn't like it. God asked why. I said that it made me feel bad. I asked God why I had to watch the video and God said *data*.

Then Dad came into my room and asked how I was feeling. God showed me a quick video of Mom driving and said *don't say anything*. I didn't say anything. Dad asked my why I didn't respond to his question and God said *say good* so I said good.

Then Dad asked if I still wanted to go to the barbeque tomorrow. I said yes and Dad said okay and left my room. Every year some of the teachers at University throw a big barbeque. We always get invited because Dad works with some of the teachers and they're kind of friends. Last year some of the English teachers cooked a goat.

But this year I was nervous. I was scared God would do something and I didn't know how to tell Dad that God was back without God hearing. God didn't say anything to me for the rest of Saturday and then I went down to the kitchen this morning and Mom and Dad were sitting at the table looking really sad. I asked what was wrong and they said that something happened at University. I asked what and they said that the police shot someone.

I didn't know what to say and it seemed like Mom and Dad didn't either because no one said anything for a long time. Then I asked if we were still going to the barbeque. Mom and Dad looked at each other and then Dad said yeah but that it probably wouldn't be very convivial and they could see if Allison was free if I didn't want to go. I asked God what convivial meant and then I thought about it and decided that I still wanted to go.

Now we're here and it's sunny but Dad was right about it not being very convivial. All the teachers are mostly talking in whispers and saying the same things to each other and no one brought a goat. Some of the teachers' kids tried to talk to me but I didn't like them and after we talked for a little bit I found a chair and sat down. God hasn't said anything since we got to the party and I haven't said anything to God but now a bunch of new people are here and they're all wearing masks. God says they're grad students so I ask God if grad students are supposed to have guns.

Tarde

Adventurists! Ambush the professors, and what? Go to jail? We need to build.

Hence the party. I am a proud member of the University Graduate Worker Liberation Front (UGWLF), recently split from the University Graduate Student Liberation Front (UGSLF), from which recently split the UGPLF (University Graduate Proletarian Liberation Front (ultraleftists)). We are all separate from the reformists at the UGSU. Lenin says,

> We have said that there could not have been Social-Democratic consciousness among the workers. It would have to be brought to them from without. The history of all countries shows that the working class, exclusively by its own effort, is able to develop only trade union consciousness, i.e., the conviction that it is necessary to combine in unions, fight the employers, and strive to compel the government to pass necessary labour legislation, etc. The theory of socialism, however, grew out of the philosophic, historical, and economic theories elaborated by educated representatives of the propertied classes, by intellectuals. By their social status the founders of modern

> scientific socialism, Marx and Engels, themselves be-
> longed to the bourgeois intelligentsia.[1]

Many of us are members of the bourgeois intelligentsia; we must not pretend to be something we are not; we are most useful to the real movement when we are acting authentically and according to our skillset. This is what Chairwoman Bisque said to me when we first decided on roles for the UGWLF. This is why I am the digital strategist.

I prefer the descriptor 'digital pedagogue' to 'digital strategist,' and per my requests, we have it earmarked to discuss nomenclature at a future date. The psychologist Catherine Almond has done fascinating research[2] on the power of names, which, while plagued by typical idealist distortions, neverthe-less contains a profound kernel of truth. Only a dogmatist would reject the theories of the bourgeois intelligentsia whole-sale; a scientific socialist must always engage in rigorous im-manent critique. This way, we may have a true revolution-ary theory—as Lenin famously said, '[w]ithout revolutionary theory there can be no revolutionary movement.'[3]

We appear to be on the verge of a revolutionary moment: an undergraduate has set herself on fire in Main Quad; a re-

---

1. V. I. Lenin, ed. V. J. Jerome, trans. J. Fineberg and G. Hanna. *What Is to Be Done?: Burning Questions of Our Movement* (New York: International Publishers, 1969), 17-18.

2. Catherine Almond. *Names and Their Uses: Nominative Determin-ism in the Twenty-First Century* (University: University University Press, 2014).

3. Lenin, *What Is to be Done*, 12.

cent graduate has been shot by the police. These are manifest tragedies, and must be treated as such; however, you may know the perhaps apocryphal Mao quote: 'everything under heaven is in utter chaos; the situation is excellent.' The party must move and it must move quickly. We must connect not just with the undergraduates, but with the workers, with the masses. We must harness their boundless creative energy and use it to build true democracy in our educational apparati; we must build.

Media theorist Roxanne Soapberry has cogently argued that the 'the memetic paraform is always already a process by which the democratization of communication necessarily imbricates itself.'[4] This is to say, we must not act unthinkingly. Chairwoman Bisque said at last night's meeting that my social media work is indispensable at this revolutionary juncture—and of this, I have little doubt. Lest we become dogmatist relics trapped in historical amber, we must find a way to harness social media's revolutionary potential. Of course, it is equally clear that the real work of revolution will not happen online; we must act, build, and organize, not simply consume. But it should be thirdly self-evident that such praxis will not happen spontaneously; we must also explicate revolutionary theory, history, and culture, and empower the masses to create their own. This is the world-historical task of the revolutionary intellectual.

And therein lies the dilemma that I currently face. As I

---

4. Roxanne Soapberry. *Form and Paraform: Media, Democracy, and the Meme* (University: University University Press, 2016), 184.

will now attempt to articulate, social media is fundamentally reactionary in character. It is, in a very real sense, diametrically opposed to the fundamentally dialectical character of revolutionary theory.

We begin with the meme. What is it? A working definition could be this: a thing that is spread between a lot of people. But this is hopelessly abstract; let us consider some examples. Consider Figure 1. It contains an example of what meme encyclopedia Know Your Meme calls the 'Expanding Brain,' or 'Galaxy Brain,' meme.

Figure 1: An example of a galaxy brain meme

The ideas are arranged in a hierarchy from worst to best; the better the idea, the more galactic the brain. The hierarchy may also be ironic. For our purposes, however, it does not matter. Instead of seeing this meme as a visual artifact, like a piece of art, I'll suggest that we take after cultural critic and theorist Erzhan Tohax and see it as a 'cognitive artifact,'[5] an externalized thought process, something like a mathematical formula. When you assess ideas, you have to do the hard work of comparing A to B, B to C, A to C, and so on, until you can line them all up yourself. But here, you, the viewer, think through the meme; as in a mathematical expression, the relationship between the values is predetermined; you simply substitute the relevant content in. All the thinking has been done for you.

Let's belabor this point with an obtuse excursus on the meme form. Consider Figure 2, what is sometimes called a 'label meme.'

Figure 2: An example of a label meme

It's a joke about Frankfurt School theorists Theodor Ador-

---

5. Erzhan Tohax. *Of Bread and Bun: Periodizing Sandwichery in the Late 20th Century* (University: University University Press, 2007), 8.

no and Max Horkheimer's essay 'The Concept of Enlightenment.' The Enlightenment was supposed to free us from myths but instead it reproduced them, just like this man is supposed to be looking at his girlfriend but instead is looking at the girl passing him. This meme is functioning as a visual metaphor. It's equating two things: labels and image.

Perhaps you fail to see the humor in jokes that reference Adorno and Horkheimer's 'The Concept of Enlightenment.' Nevertheless, you observe that the meme has great comedic potential. So you create a new meme, found in Figure 3.

Figure 3: Another example of a label meme

A joke about Adorno and Horkheimer's essay 'The Culture Industry' is better, but of course, it's entirely possible that someone else now sees your meme and my meme and, seeing an avenue through which to unleash the boundless river of human creativity, creates a few more memes; these, in turn, are seen, riffed on, so on and so forth.

Here is the essential question: is there an equality relationship between the content of your meme, my meme, and all the rest of the memes? Recall we claimed that one meme was equating two things, A (the labels) to B (the image). And if the next meme is equating C (the new labels) to B (the same image), and the one after that is equating D (the new, new labels) to B (the same image), then A, C, and D should all share something in common: namely, that they can be expressed through B, the Distracted Boyfriend meme. This means we can abstract them all into the same organizing structure (the same 'meme'). Here, that structure is: something, the thing it should X, the thing it is actually X-ing. Let us also think about this like a mathematical expression we can use to relate content; the relationship between the variables doesn't change, although the values of the variables might. In fact, we can have two contradicting versions of the meme. Imagine one where the boy is labeled 'the youth,' one girl says 'communism,' and the other girl says 'capitalism'—now reverse them. Note the epistemological confusion: we are being deceived by top-down thinking.

I could provide more examples, however, Chairwoman Bisque has suggested that I practice the art of concision, and as theorist György Lukács says, '[t]he proletariat must not shy away from self-criticism, for victory can only be gained by the truth and self-criticism must, therefore, be its natural element.'[6]

So let us proceed with brevity. Adorno and Horkheimer

---

6. György Lukács, trans. Rodney Livingstone. *History and Class Consciousness: Studies in Marxist Dialectics*. (Cambridge, MA: MIT Press, 1999), 81.

claim that Enlightenment thought works by making 'dissimilar things comparable by reducing them to abstract quantities;'[7] thus 'nature, stripped of qualities, becomes the chaotic stuff of mere classification.'[8] In the Enlightenment system, 'whatever might be different is made the same. That is the verdict which critically sets the boundaries to possible experience.'[9] Memes work similarly. We can make memes out of novel content, but this is tantamount to saying that the content is not so novel. We expose something new (novel content) as something old (meme structure)—and this, I contend, is what Adorno and Horkheimer mean by 'myth.' If it is true that 'the regression of the masses today lies in their inability to hear with their own ears what has not already been heard, to touch with their hands what has not previously been grasped,'[10] then perhaps the memetic mode of thinking is a part of it.

This all, perhaps, seems alien to the concerns of revolutionary socialists, but I'll suggest that it is not. I'll suggest that many purported revolutionary socialists think in precisely this fashion: beginning with an abstract concept or structure and using it to interpret the historical situation they find themselves in. But revolutionary theory loses its revolutionary char-

---

7. Theodor W. Adorno and Max Horkheimer, ed. Gunzelin Schmid Noerr, trans. Edmund Jephcott. *Dialectic of Enlightenment: Philosophical Fragments*. (Stanford, CA: Stanford University Press, 2002), 9.

8. Ibid, 6.

9. Ibid, 8.

10. Ibid, 29.

acter when it begins with the theory; it must always begin with the concrete particulars of the historical situation it is meant to describe. Reality takes precedence. Theory can always be updated; indeed, it should be. Otherwise, it is simply dogma. And dogma, like the meme, makes for decent propaganda and bad pedagogy.

I have attempted to explain all of this to Chairwoman Bisque, but it is her and the rest of the party's contention that decent propaganda is more necessary at this revolutionary juncture than good pedagogy, and that given my skills at creating the former, and track record of attempts at the latter, it is best I simply follow the dictates of democratic centralism and do as I am told.

So I have been agitating online. Feed is down, but the other platforms remain. I have slept very little, and except for a brief foray into the hallways and courtyard to help look for my roommate's missing pet, I have not left my computer. I am in hell.

I mean that chronotopically. Literary theorist Mikhail Bakhtin defines a *chronotope* in the following way: '[w]e will give the name chronotope (literally, "time space") to the intrinsic connectedness of temporal and spatial relationships that are artistically expressed in literature . . . What counts for us is the fact that it expresses the inseparability of space and time.'[11] As illustration, consider the chronotope in which Bakhtin finds 'the unity of time and space markers is exhibited with excep-

---

11. Mikhail Bakhtin, ed. Michael Holquist, trans. Caryl Emerson and Michael Holquist. *The Dialogic Imagination.* (Austin: University of Texas Press, 2010), 84.

tional precision and clarity:'[12] the road. On the road, the 'course of an individual's life' is fused 'with his actual spatial course or road—that is, with his wanderings. So we get the metaphor "the path of life."'[13] Let us consider some ordinary expressions we often use to describe where we are in life: 'I'm at a crossroads,' 'directionless,' 'going nowhere.' We should see that, even in the phrase 'where we are in life,' there's an obviously spatial dimension to the way we imagine the temporality of our lives.

This is significant; consider this thought in the context of what literary theorist Fredric Jameson calls a *cognitive map*. The idea of a cognitive map is itself Jameson's rework of Kevin Lynch's idea that 'the alienated city is above all a space in which people are unable to map (in their minds) either their own positions or the urban totality in which they find themselves;' what the 'cognitive map is called upon to do in the narrower framework of daily life in the physical city' is 'enable a situational representation on the part of the individual subject to that vaster and properly unrepresentable totality which is the ensemble of society's structures as a whole.'[14]

Our cognitive map is how we relate to our spatial environment. Above, we looked at some idioms we use to relate to our temporal environment; they were all spatio-temporal. So let's imagine there is something called a *cognitive chronotope*,

---

12. Ibid, 98.

13. Ibid, 120.

14. Fredric Jameson. *Postmodernism, or, the Cultural Logic of Late Capitalism*. (Durham: Duke University Press, 1991), 25.

which is the way we map our personal position, and our collective position, in the temporal totality: history. Even though spatially the road of life can go every which way—'they're doing some wandering,' 'she's taken some turns,' 'he's fallen off the path'—I'll submit that the baseline we imagine these deviations from is a simple form: a horizontal line, literally a life span (Figure 4).

Figure 4: A life span, or timeline

This is the same form we see in our earliest classes about history: the timeline. We arrange a series of events horizontally, from past to present. Here is an important claim: horizontal movement through time is the formal way in which we imagine diachronicity. *Diachronic* thinking is concerned with the way something changes through time, and even in the word *through*, we can sense that there's a horizontal movement being imagined.[15]

Why might this matter? Consider that the chronotope is simply one of many examples of what literary theorist Caroline Levine calls *form*: 'form always indicates an arrangement of elements—*an ordering, patterning, or shaping*,' which for

---

15. I'll submit this is because of numbers, which we use to mark time, and which, at least in the system of math we use today, are put on a number line. If you say that X was one way at time marker 1, and another way at time marker 5, it's understood that between then, X was also a certain way at time 2, 3, and 4—and notice the spatial language when we say between 1 and 5, and the horizontal movement it implies.

her and for us 'will mean all shapes and configurations, all ordering principles, all patterns of repetition and difference.'[16] Given this tremendously encompassing definition of form, it is a good idea to ask: why does it matter that something is or isn't a form? One answer is it does not; what matters is what a form *affords*, a term Levine lifts from design theory that's "used to describe the potential uses or actions latent in materials and designs."[17] Just as a material or design allows you to do certain things (chair → sit, rubber → bend), so too does a form—so too does a chronotope.

My contention is that different cognitive chronotopes afford different ways of conceptualizing our place in time and, more relevant to us, history. In her work *The Politics of Everybody*, theorist Holly Lewis claims that '[d]ialectics implies that historical time moves in one direction, that it is never possible to reverse its course towards an earlier stage of history. Hegelian dialecticians imagine the world moves in a spiral formation: what might look like a return is actually an advance,' a view shared by other dialecticians Veronica Cuy,[18] Augusto Egusi,[19] and Vladimir Lenin.[20]

---

16. Caroline Levine. *Forms: Whole, Rhythm, Hierarchy, Network*. (Princeton: Princeton University Press, 2015), 3.

17. Ibid, 6.

18. Veronica Cuy, trans. Rosa Anticucho. *Capital and Knowledge*. (New York: Yearly Review Press, 1975), 107.

19. Augusto Egusi, ed. Moses Hog Sr. *Egusi's Collected Speeches*. (University: University University Press, 2004), 279.

20. V. I. Lenin, ed. Stewart Smith, trans. Clemence Dutt. *Lenin's Collected Works*, 4th English Edition. Volume 38. (Moscow: Progress Publishers,

If the spiral enables us to imagine historical progress, albeit, as Jameson says, 'on its left foot, as it were, progressing, as Henri Lefebvre once put it, by way of catastrophe and disaster,'[21] then I'll suggest that the cognitive chronotope embodied by social media, the dominant form of the feed, seen and lived in by billions of workers worldwide, is one of temporal and historical stasis. Consider Figure 5, the form of social media.

Figure 5: The form of social media

This affords nothing in the way of historical progress; it is hell:

> a world that has its life and movement tensely strung
> along a vertical axis: nine circles of Hell beneath the
> earth, seven circles of Purgatory above them and above

1965), 245, 361.

21. Jameson, *Postmodernism*, xi.

that ten circles of Paradise....The temporal logic of this vertical world consists in the sheer simultaneity of all that occurs (or "the coexistence of everything in eternity"). Everything that on earth is divided by time, here, in this verticality, coalesces into eternity, into pure simultaneous coexistence. Such divisions as time introduces—"earlier" and "later" have no substance here; they must be ignored in order to understand this vertical world; everything must be perceived as being within a single time, that is, in the synchrony of a single moment; one must see this entire world as simultaneous.[22]

So, we may conclude, in both content (meme) and form (feed), social media is deeply reactionary. As in hell, here we experience a temporal logic that consists in the 'sheer simultaneity of all that occurs,'[23] as Bakhtin puts it, or 'an experience of pure material signifiers, or, in other words, a series of pure and unrelated presents in time,'[24] as Jameson does. This temporal logic is quite literally perpendicular to the temporal logic of diachronic thinking that we saw in Figure 4. The cultural logic of late capitalism, here embodied by the indisputably dominant form of social media, condemns us to a vertical axis, to stasis.

You'll observe that this is all neatly encapsulated by a common leftist academic orthodoxy, 'it is easier to imagine the

---

22. Bakhtin, *The Dialogic Imagination*, 157.

23. Ibid.

24. Jameson, *Postmodernism*, 26.

end of the world than it is to imagine the end of capitalism.'[25] I prefer another popular thesis, sometimes attributed to Malcolm X: 'we are not outnumbered; we are out-organized.' We do not need imaginary socialism; we have real capitalism. As Karl Marx says, 'we do not attempt dogmatically to prefigure the future, but want to find the new world only through criticism of the old.'[26]

Perhaps you will see what the party does not. If the workers of the world are to fulfill their world-historical task, they—we—must break free from this stasis. We must build. It is true, everything under heaven is in utter chaos, but is it not, as Audre Lorde has it, 'out of Chaos that new worlds are born?'[27]

25. Mark Fisher. *Capitalist Realism: Is there no alternative?*. (Zer0 Books, 2009), 2

26. Friedrich Engels and Karl Marx, ed. Robert C. Tucker. *The Marx-Engels Reader*. (New York: Norton, 1972), 13.

27. Audre Lorde. "Eye to Eye: Black Women, Hatred, and Anger." *Sister Outsider: Essays and Speeches*. (New York: Crossing Press, 2012), 162.

The One about the Horny Lesbian Crab

I'm free and I'm going to fuck. I just have to find some she-crab. It shouldn't be that hard. I'm a top.

My old owner doesn't really fuck. She spends most of her nights high and on Wikipedia. I've heard her explain the lack of fucking to her roommate; it was convoluted. I think it probably has less to do with 'ontologies of desire' and more to do with the fact that she still dresses like a fifteen-year-old boy that doesn't know she's a fifteen-year-old girl. Her roommate isn't getting much either. At least they have the party. I could have easily fucked enough for the three of us, but there was the issue of the cage. It's really a tossup who did the most yearning. God I miss fucking. God I miss the sea.

Wikipedia is how she learned about certain cancrine divination rituals, which is how I came to live in the cage. I don't know anything about cancrine divination, and neither does she, but it was fun to pretend, at least for a while. Then, last night, she got too high and left the cage unlocked. Now I'm free.

So I've been scuttling towards the eXe campus. I figure they'll have live crabs there, in the kitchen. I just have to break in and free them.

I've been scuttling all night. I'm tired. But it'll be worth it. Feeling that scrape against my shell. I can't wait.

I've decided that no one here fucks. That's the vibe I'm getting. At least from the clothes. They have sex, probably. But no one really fucks. I'm sure they think it's because they think too much. A life of the mind. But I think plenty. I just also fuck. They're not really opposed. It's just an energy thing.

Everything here is basically a theme park, is what it is. That's the only reason I'm here. Because she read something she thought sounded cool and decided to recreate it. They're all just recreating. And that's why they can never fuck. Because fucking would involve too much zero-order experience. It would also involve too much sex, something I think these people might only have if you wrang it out of them. And then it wouldn't be sex. Because it wouldn't ooze.

At least that's how it works in the sea. Here, who knows?

I think I'm finally on the eXe campus. I can tell because the people here seem like they fuck even less. This building has a big C out front. C for crab. I think I'll try to go through an air vent or something. It looks like I need a badge to get in the front door. And this way I won't get stomped.

Fuck.

I'm so horny I think I might literally die.

But I'm in the air vents. Eventually I'll find the kitchen. I can see into their little rooms through the grates. I'm not sure why people are here today. It's Sunday. But here they are. Click clacking away. They don't seem too happy about it either. Sounds like there's a little tiff going on in this room.

— How did it get there?

— I don't know how it got there.

— What do you mean you don't know?

— I mean I don't know. They weren't there, and then they were there. Maybe it downloaded them.

— What possible reason could it have to download a dozen Summer Skye videos?

— I don't know! I didn't do it.

— It's supposed to be child safe. We wrote it to be child safe.

— We wrote it to learn.

— . . .

— . . .

— Eve is pinging me . . . fucking hell.

— Good luck.

— Yeah, thanks.

They split. One's out of there, the other to her computer.

As much as I'd love to linger, I've got places to be. But fuck these vents are confusing. And it's so cold. No wonder they're all dressed like that.

Left.

Right.

Left again.

More yelling. I think I'm lost.

— You said KtZ wasn't real.

— I assure you it is not.

— Then what the fuck am I looking at?

— I implore you-

— No, don't implore me. Explain. Explain how the fuck all of this got here!

— Surely you have considered the possibility that Feed is retaliating.

— They haven't even had twenty-four hours!

— I would assume they have someone on the inside, so to speak.

— Why would you assume that?

— You do.

— . . .

— . . .

— This is a mess, this is such a fucking mess. You said we would take down Feed.

— And we did.

I swear to god I'm going to die. I'm literally going to die.

But we move.

Right.

Right.

Left.

Right.

Straight.

Left.

Oh huh . . .

— No one knows, Eve! That's what I'm saying.

— This is Eliot's kid we're talking about.

— I know that. I know that.

— And now I can't even get a hold of him.

— Fucking hell.

— He said it was ready.

Boring.

Left.

Right.

Right.

Left.

Straight.

Left.

Hmm. This guy again.

— All in all, I would say it was a measured success, Joshua.

A measured success.

— Did you get a chance to look at the Soufflé data?

— This morning. Nothing but idealist dreck. Useless.

— That's a shame.

— What's one to a planet?

— Two with John.

— That couldn't be avoided.

— Fair enough.

— You removed the sound system from the trees?

— It's with the payphone and the gun.

— Good man.

Left.

Straight.

Straight.

Left.

Straight.

— Why the fuck did we agree to this?

— Data.

— Right.

— Money.

— Right.

Left.

Right.

Right.

Right.

Right.

Left.

— Listen to me! That video is generated. They used the Turrón function, okay? The note too. You train an LLM on a bunch of canonical literature . . . I don't have time to explain what an LLM is . . . it's just . . . it's all experimental tech, AGI, nanobiotics, that kid they shot, you have to believe me, you have to fucking believe me.

Straight.

Left.

Left.

Straight.

Wait how the fuck am I back . . .

— It's a pity it didn't come out better.

— You didn't like it? I thought it read well.

— Had we the time.

— So now what?

— Now we wait.

Straight.

Straight.

Straight.

Left.

Right.

Left.
Oh shit! This must be the cafeteria.
Fuck that's a lot of crab.

Deepo

It's short for the Decomposer. That's what my boys call me. Deepo. The Decomposer. Basically I've got this thing I do whenever we order food to share because we always order too much and there's always some left and everyone's full and I'm full but I'm looking at the food and I'm thinking, someone should finish that, and it's getting later and later and the food's getting cold and you know the lo mein's like congealing and you stick the chopsticks in and you get this like trapezoidal block or like pizza, pizza's the fucking worst, I can do some damage on a lukewarm pizza. And like I'm full you know. It's just like I could eat more. I can always eat more. It's bad bro, it's bad. I'll eat shit that's straight up frigid, it doesn't matter, I'll be standing in front of the fridge eating whole pieces of cold chicken, picking it out with my hands, I won't even be thinking about it, just standing there and eating this cold chicken breast and just fucking hating myself but I can't stop, you know, I can never stop. And it's not even like I'm really feeling that hungry all the time. I can just always eat more. So my friends call me Deepo. They think it's funny. And it kind of is. But like. It's not like I haven't tried to stop. I've tried all sorts of shit. In high school I convinced one of my moms to buy me smaller plates, all so I would feel like I was eating more food, like I could just trick my stomach into thinking it was full. Nope. Just ate more servings. Tried drinking water. Tried drinking tea. Tried drinking coffee. I've even straight up tried pills. Had a buddy of mine order some off the dark web. Sitting there fucking tweaking. And for what? Only one thing has worked and I'm not even sure it worked. It's not like lifting made me eat less. Maybe it made me eat more. But it made me feel okay about eating. See that's the thing about lifting. You're not overeating, you're bulking. You're not undereating, you're cutting. You're not eating normally, you're eating at maintenance. Just totally warps the way you think about food. Especially if you're trying to track your macros. That changes the calculus. Monastic eating. Chicken and broccoli. Every day of the week. No joke. I've seen this shit online; they'll make seven courses of it on a Sunday and that's their whole week. Chicken and broccoli. Identical tupperware. Every day. It cannot be healthy bro. Like psychically. That shit has to be damaging. And it's sick, you know. I don't want to feel bad about eating. I love it. Like food, like cooking, like the whole history, the culture, it's all beautiful. That's the thing. But I feel bad man I feel so fucking bad. I can't stop. I just go. To pain. Physical fucking pain. It hurts. It hurts to be like this. Like today my boy brings me to eXe because he says the cafeteria's open and we can score some free food and whatever, it's been a rough weekend I could use some fancy tech people food so I go and I just fucking consume. I can't even count how many crabs I've eaten. Just sitting here cracking and slurping. Cracking and slurping. I just keep going. People have started to notice too. The people here. I can tell, I can fucking tell. The way they watch you eat. Do not look at me like that. I can't control this. My buddy's starting to kind of nudge me. Like hey Deepo you're really fucking steamrolling through these crabs. What do you want from me? I'm trying to stop. But I am stuck. I am in ice. I am not moving.

Me, Us, Dusk

My therapist says my problem is I'm too autobiographical. Her thing is basically that I can't really experience anything without simultaneously thinking about how to transform that experience into something someone else can consume, so what ends up happening is that I end up being both the character being presented and the author hyperconsciously manipulating that presentation to create a certain image in the other person's head, and that while it's true that most everyone in the world does this, some people do it too much, too intensely, and too neurotically, and that those people, people like me, end up being not only fundamentally incapable of experiencing anything in the world on its own terms but fundamentally incapable of experiencing themselves on their own terms, in other words, they experience everything, including their own self, at a level of abstraction and remove that prevents them from ever fully experiencing anything, ever authentically experiencing anything, ever being real, and that what all this abstract, conceptual maneuvering really sums to, at the end of the day, is a near-total inability to abide being read; I told her that's probably all true but not really that high on my list of problems, and she asked me what was on my list of problems, and I told her suicide, and she told me that there was a sense in which, transitioning, I had already committed a kind of suicide, to which I legitimately had nothing to say; maybe I need a new therapist.

But I thought about what she was saying for a while, and I realized she's kind of right. Not about the trans stuff, but the rest. I can write you in, but I can't write me out. I thought about that for a while, and then I decided that I would buy a big enough pot and cook myself into a giant soup—so now I'm here, waiting in the water. I don't know why I decided I would do it at University. It's my world, I guess . . .

. . . ours, too. She's one of us now. Get ready; we don't have much time: it's dusk, and a lot has been happening off-screen. The entrances to the University campus have been blocked; police barricades stand opposite protesters, thousands of whom have assembled here, coming in from the surrounding towns, the nearby cities, the other schools; inside, the students appear quiet, beaten down.

But appearances can be deceiving; a trio of enterprising University freshmen have figured out how to access the police radio waves, and now reports of property damage are luring them to all the wrong places, allowing the rest of the students to emerge from their supposed slumber and converge on Main Quad—so . . . riot? Haven't they heard enough screams? Maybe it's time to break some shit. The English building, the Math building, the President's second office, all suitable candidates for a little torching: Chip's ready, and Nat brought a lighter; the roommates are primed; the showerers are open;

Ana Turrón's thinking ahead, wondering how she can use her talents for Good; even the Degenerates have turned out—all our friends in one place. We hope you'll forgive our excitement; it's just some of us have been here a long time. We've seen students come and go. Burn. Smolder. Extinguish. But nothing like this. What are you supposed to do while your world eats itself alive? Take notes? You have time: neither revolution nor ruin will happen overnight, nice though it is to imagine they could: you wake up one morning, and help has arrived: wars have ended, surplus value has been returned, services have been built, prisons have closed, the police have stopped murdering people. The earth escapes only a little toasted. Or maybe you luck out, and, in one swift act of ecokarmic retribution, it's burnt to a crisp. You don't wake up at all— at least it was quick. No, instead you have time: you can get used to things. Do you feel powerless? Most of us do. Capitalism, so the thinking goes, is both an unstoppable force and an immovable object. It takes a certain level of delusion to think otherwise, one you'd imagine would be impossible to sustain. But it is very difficult to forget the feeling of the world cracking open. Nothing compares. We often understand radicalization in negative terms, ruptured illusions and properly perceived realities—where were you when you realized how the world truly is? But where were you when you saw a police station burn down? Where were you when you accepted that everything could change? That everything is already changing. It's war, isn't it: not life versus death, or human versus system, but class against class, human versus human. Everyone picks a side. So why pick the losers? More than half of these students already come from the top ten percent of American wealth; the rest could get there. Why burn what's theirs? Why commit a kind of suicide?

What else is there?

Right now, there is only tonight. Revolution won't happen here, but something could. Everyone's present. The students. The outside protesters. Now the police. It's here. Now. And something has to break.

Well—

Acknowledgments

Many thanks to Avery D'Agostino for their careful proofreading and to Zhanpei Fang for the beautiful cover art.

Thank you, too, to the various teachers and mentors I've had who have taught me how to think about art, especially: Mo Harry, Brad Sharp, Corey Snyder, Jason Flowers, Nina Schloesser Tárano, NoViolet Bulawayo, Haydn Middleton, Nicholas Friedman, Elizabeth Tallent, Sibongile Sithe, John Bender, Mark McGurl, Vaughn Rasberry, Shannon Pufahl, and Johnny Walker.

I've also learned a lot about artistry from my friends in the Tolliver Collective, as well as from a brilliant collection of writers I shared this work with: Kion You, Tom Cusano, Nate Brown, Thayer Anderson, Anna Sudderth, and Oriana Tang. Thank you all!

A lot of other friends read pieces of the book and supported me through this process. A giant thank you to Nathan Weiser, Camila Novo-Viaño, Mark Mendoza, Courtney Pal, Michael Zhu, Gabby Schreiner, Dri Esparza, Ena Alvarado, Feroz James, Frank Feder, Michael Zhou, Evan Pandya, Ada Statler, Mohit Mookim, Graeme Hewett, Katherine Uhlman,

Spencer Slovic, Phoebe Oathout, Stephanie Wang, Abigail Schott-Rosenfield, Sophie Clark, Janna Huang, Ben Spar, Niall Chithelen, Liz Chadwick, Frances Saux, Dana Dzik, Kali Koba, and Maks Bondarenko.

I couldn't have written this book without my family. Thank you to Ruchi Gupta, David Freed, Dan Freed, and Sonia Pabán.

And finally, thank you to Claudia McKenzie. You make everything possible.